# Timberland
# Writes
# Together

"Ice in D Minor" © 2015 Anthea Sharp
"Something to Sneeze At" © 2015 Jim Tweedie
"Heart's Delight" © 2015 Pam Anderson
"Christmas, 1957" © 2015 Keith Eisner
"Going Without" © 2015 Meagan Macvie
"Mistakes Are Made" © 2015 Caelyn Williams
"Hush, Now" © 2014 Beth Anderson. Originally published in
    *The Saturday Evening Post*. Reprinted by permission of the author.
"Ordinary Housework" © 2015 Laura Koerber
"What on Fleem" © 2015 Edward Marcus
"The Prince Phillip Hotel" © 2015 Suzanne Staples
"Neighbors" © 2015 Llyn De Danaan
"Whiteout" © 2015 Eve Hambruch
"Relatively Well" © 2015 Jessie Weaver
"The Fire Finder" © 2015 Barbara Yunker
"The Strandweaver" © 2015 Kim K. O'Hara

Cover illustration "The Thing with Feathers" © 2015 Kathryn Wanless

Published by Timberland Regional Library
www.TRL.org

ISBN-13: 978-1516960347
ISBN-10: 1516960343

# Timberland

# Writes

# Together

Timberland Regional
LIBRARY

Kathryn Wanless was born and raised in England, and is largely a self-taught artist. Her passion is for telling stories through words, pictures and theatre. Her artwork is primarily inspired by her love for children's literature, poetry and the art nouveau movement.

She has a degree in linguistics from University College London, where she also took several drawing classes at the Slade School of Fine Art. After graduating, she worked as an English instructor in France and Prague before moving to Olympia, Washington ten years ago.

Here in Washington she has taught high school art and drama, created commissioned paintings and illustrations for local churches and businesses, directed plays, acted in numerous local theatre productions, and is always happy to doodle greetings cards for friends.

Kathryn currently lives in Olympia with her husband, two little girls and one labrador. She is a full-time mother, part-time baker, and a some-of-the-time writer and artist. She hopes to continue to pursue her lifelong dream of writing and illustrating for children.

# Contents

# Introduction

One year ago, the Timberland Regional Library's (TRL) Board of Trustees enthusiastically approved an exciting project suggested by a TRL employee: to promote and celebrate the artists among us by publishing a collection of regional writing and art. You are holding the result of that idea in your hands, the *Timberland Writes Together* anthology.

The number of submissions of short fiction and cover art far exceeded our expectations. After many long sessions of reading and deliberation, fifteen stories and one work of art were selected.

The call for submissions went out in early January. We asked only that the stories and art reflect a sense of optimism. Everything else was left up to the creativity of the writers and artists. This call yielded work from 198 writers and artists — over 696,000 words of fiction and 91 pieces of artwork. For some, this was the first time they had submitted work for publication.

This October, our community will reconvene for the 16th annual "Timberland Reads Together" a month-long, "one book, one community" reading program. The program focus will be the *Timberland Writes Together* anthology. Throughout the 27 libraries across five counties, people will gather for book and panel discussions, author readings, writing workshops, and sessions on how local writers can become published authors.

Works of fiction, such as those in this anthology, allow us to live different lives, glimpse different realities and experience other ways of thinking.

Enjoy,

Cheryl Heywood
Library Director
June 2015

Growing up on fairy tales and computer games,
Anthea Sharp has melded the two in her USA
Today bestselling Feyland fantasy series.
She makes her home in the Pacific Northwest,
where she writes, hangs out in virtual worlds,
plays the fiddle with her Celtic band Fiddlehead,
and spends time with her small-but-good family.

In addition to penning award-winning Science
Fantasy, Anthea is also a bestselling author of
historical romance under the pen name Anthea
Lawson. Her novels have won or placed in the
PRISM, the RITA, the National Reader's Choice
Award, the Write Touch Reader's Award, the
Heart of Excellence, The National Excellence
in Romance Fiction, The Judge a Book by its
Cover, and the Book Buyer's Best contests.

# Ice in D Minor

Rinna Sen paced backstage, tucking her mittened hands deep into the pockets of her parka. The sound of instruments squawking to life cut through the curtains screening the front of the theater: the sharp cry of a piccolo, the heavy thump of tympani, the whisper and saw of forty violins warming up. *Good luck with that.* Despite the huge heaters trained on the open-air proscenium, the North Pole in February was *cold.*

And about to get colder, provided she did her job.

The stage vibrated slightly, balanced in the center of a parabolic dish pointed straight up to the distant specks of stars in the frigid black sky. The stars floated impossibly far away — but they weren't the goal. No, her music just had to reach the thermo-acoustic engine hovering ten miles above the earth, centered over the pole.

Rinna breathed in, shards of cold stabbing her lungs. Her blood longed for summer in Mumbai; the spice-scented air that pressed heat into skin, into bone, so deeply a body wanted to collapse under the impossible weight and lie there, baking, under the blue sky.

That had been in her childhood. Now, nobody lived in the searing swath in the center of the globe. The heat between the tropics had become death to the human organism.

Not to mention that her home city was now under twenty feet of water. There was no going back, ever.

"Ms. Sen?" Her assistant, Dominic Larouse, hurried up, his nose constantly dripping from the chill. "There's a problem with the tubas."

Rinna sighed — a puff of breath, visible even in the dim air. "What, their lips are frozen to the mouthpieces? I told them to bring plastic ones."

"Valve issues, apparently."

Dominic dabbed his nose with his ever-present handkerchief. He'd been with her for two years, and she still couldn't break through his stiff formality. But little things, like insisting on being called by her first name, weren't worth the aggravation. Not here, not now.

"Get more heaters on them," she said, "and tell those damn violins we start in five minutes, whether they're warmed up or not."

"Five minutes. Yes ma'am."

Her job included being a hardass, but she knew how difficult it was to keep the instruments on pitch. The longer they waited, the worse it would get.

Goddess knew, they'd tried this the easy way by feeding remote concerts into the climate engine. Ever since the thing was built, the scientists had been trying to find the right frequencies to cool the atmosphere. They'd had the best luck with minor keys — something about the energy transfer — and at first had tried running synthesized pitches through. Then entire performances. Mozart's Requiem had come close, but not close enough.

It had to be a live performance; the immediate, present sounds of old wood, horsehair, brass and felt, the cascade of subtle human imperfection, blown and pulled and pounded from the organic bodies of the instruments.

There was no substitute for the interactions of sound waves, the immeasurable atomic collisions of an on-site concert fed directly into the engine. Once the thing got started, the techs had promised they could loop the sound. Which was good, because no way was Rinna giving up the rest of her life to stand at the North Pole, conducting a half-frozen orchestra. Not even to save the planet.

She'd spent years working on her composition, assembled the best symphony in the world, rehearsed them hard, then brought them here, to the Arctic. Acoustic instruments and sub-zero temperatures didn't get along, but damn it, she'd make this happen.

*What if the composition is a failure?* The voice of all her doubts ghosted through her thoughts, sounding suspiciously like her long-dead father.

She pinned it down and piled her answers on top, trying to smother it into silence.

The simulations had proven that certain frequencies played through the engine could super-cool the air over the pole. Then, with luck, a trickle-down effect would begin and slowly blanket the world.

The scientists had run the models over and over, with a thousand different types of sound. But it wasn't until the suits had hired Rinna — one of the best composers in the world (not that the world cared much about symphonies) — that the project had really started to gel.

"Ms. Sen." Dominic hurried up again, holding out the slim screen of her tablet. "Vid call for you."

"I told you, I don't want any interruptions."

"It's the President."

"Oh, very well." Fingers clumsy through her mittens, Rinna took the call.

President Nishimoto, Leader of the Ten Nations of the World, smiled at her through the clear, bright screen. Behind him, the desert that used to be Moscow was visible through the window of his office.

"Ms. Sen," he said. "The entire world wishes you the very best of luck in your performance."

He didn't need to say how much was at stake. They all knew.

"Thank you." She bowed, then handed the screen back to Dominic.

It was almost too late. Last winter, the pole ice had thinned so much it couldn't support the necessary installation. Doom criers had mourned the end, but a freak cold-snap in January had given them one final chance.

Now here they were — the orchestra, the techs, Rinna. And five thousand brave, stupid souls, camping on the precarious ice. Come to see the beginning of the world, or the end of it.

Out front, the oboe let out an undignified honk, then found the *A*. Rinna closed her eyes as the clear pitch rang out, quieting the rest of the musicians. The violins took it up, bows pulling, tweaking, until there was only one perfect, single note. It deepened as the lower strings joined in, cellos and basses rounding the *A* into a solid arc of octaves.

She could feel the dish magnifying the vibration, up through her feet. Sound was powerful. Music could change the world. She had to believe that.

As the strings quieted, Rinna stripped off her mittens, then lifted her conductor's baton from its velvet-lined case. The polished mahogany grip was comfortable in her hand, despite the chill. The stick itself was carved of mammoth ivory, dug out of the ground centuries ago.

She ran her fingers up and down the smooth white length. It was fitting, using a relic of an extinct animal in this attempt to keep humans from going out the same way.

She stepped onstage, squinting in the stage lights, as the wind instruments began to tune. First the high silver notes of the flutes, then the deep, mournful call of the French horns and low brass. Sounded like the tubas had gotten themselves sorted out.

From up here, the ice spread around stage — not pale and shimmering under the distant stars, but dark and clotted with onlookers. Originally, she'd imagined performing to the quiet, blank landscape — but that was before some brilliantly wacko entrepreneur had started selling tickets and chartering boats into the bitter reaches of the North.

The concert of a lifetime, plus the novelty of cold, drew spectators from all over the planet. No doubt the thrill of the chill had worn off, but the performance, the grand experiment, was still to come.

And truthfully, Rinna was glad for the crowd. Thermo-acoustics aside, she knew from long experience that the energy of playing in front of responsive listeners was *different*. Call it physics, call it woo-woo, but the audience was an integral part of the performance.

The project director had been reluctant at first, constructing only a small shelter and selling tickets at prices she didn't even want to contemplate. The enclosed seating held roughly forty people: heads of state, classical music aficionados, those with enough money and sense to try and stay warm. But when the boats started arriving, the tents going up, what could he do?

The spectators all wanted to be here, with the possible exception of Dominic hovering beside the podium.

The crowd caught sight of her striding across the stage, and applause rushed like a wind over the flat, frigid plain. She lifted her hand in acknowledgement. Overhead, the edge of the aurora flickered, a pale fringe of light.

Rinna stepped onto the podium and looked over her orchestra, illuminated by white spotlights and the ruddy glow of the heaters.

She'd bribed and bullied and called in every favor owed her, and this was the result. The best symphony orchestra the entire world could offer. Rehearsals had been the Tower of Babel: Hindi, Chinese,

English, French — over a dozen nationalities stirred together in a cacophonous soup. But the moment they started playing, they had one perfect language in common.

Music.

The orchestra quieted. One hundred and five pairs of eyes fixed on her, and Rinna swallowed back the quick burst of nausea that always accompanied her onto the podium. The instant she lifted her baton and scribed the downbeat, it would dissipate. Until then, she'd fake feeling perfectly fine.

"Dominic?" she called, "are the techs ready?"

"Yes," he said.

"Blow your nose." No point in marring the opening with the sound of his sniffles.

Pasting a smile on her face, Rinna turned and bowed to the listeners spread out below the curve of the stage. They applauded, sparks of excitement igniting like distant firecrackers.

She pulled in a deep breath, winced as the air stabbed her lungs, and faced the orchestra — all her brave, dedicated musicians poised on the cusp of the most important performance of their lives.

The world premiere of *Ice*.

The air quieted. Above the orchestra a huge amplifier waited, a tympanic membrane ready to take the sound and feed it into the engine, transmute it to frigidity.

Rinna raised her arms, and the musicians lifted their instruments, their attention focused on her like iron on a magnet. She was their true north. The baton lay smoothly in her right hand — her talisman, her magic wand. If there ever was wizardry in the world, let it come to her now.

Heart beating fast, she let her blood set the tempo and flicked her stick upward. Then down, irrevocably down, into the first beat of *Ice*.

A millisecond of silence, and then the violins slid up into a melodic line colored with aching, while the horns laid down a base solid enough to carry the weight of the stars. The violas took the melody, letting the violins soar into descant. The hair on the back of her neck lifted at the eerie balance. Yes. Perfect. Now the cellos — too loud. She pushed the sound down slightly with her left hand, and the section followed, blending into the waves of music that washed up and up.

Rinna beckoned to the harp, and a glissando swirled out, a shimmering net cast across dark waters. Was it working? She didn't dare glance up.

High overhead, the thermo-acoustic engine waited, the enormous tubes and filters ready to take her music and make it corporeal — a thrumming machine built to restore the balance of the world.

It was crazy. It was their best chance.

*Ice* was not a long piece. It consisted of only one movement, designed along specific, overlapping frequencies. Despite its brevity, it had taken her three years to compose, working with the weather simulations and the best scientific minds in the world. Then testing on small engines, larger ones, until she stood here.

Now Rinna gestured and pulled, molded and begged, and the orchestra gave. Tears glazed her vision, froze on her lashes, but it didn't matter. She wasn't working from a score; the music lived in her body, more intimately known to her than her own child.

The clarinets sobbed the melody, grieving for what was already lost. The polar bears. The elephants. The drowned cities. The silenced birds.

Now the kettle-drums, a gradual thunder—raising the old magic, working up to the climax. The air throbbed and keened as Rinna rose onto her toes and lifted her hands higher. Higher. A divine plea.

*Save us.*

Arms raised high, Rinna held the symphony in her grasp, squeezed its heart for one more drop of musical blood. The musicians gave, faces taut with effort, shiny with sweat even in the chill. Bows flew, a faint sparkle of rosin dust flavoring the air. The trumpets blared, not missing the triad the way they had in rehearsal.

The last note. Hold. Hold. Hold.

She slashed her hand through the air and the sound stopped. *Ice* ended, yearning and dissonant, the final echo ringing into the frigid sky.

Above, nothing but silence.

Rinna lowered her arms and rocked back on her heels. From the corner of her eye, she saw the techs gesturing frantically, heads shaking, expressions grim.

The bitter taste of failure crept into her mouth, even as the crowd erupted into shouts and applause, a swell of sound washing up and over the open stage. She turned and gave them an empty bow, then gestured to the symphony — the musicians who had given and given. For nothing.

They stood, and one over-exuberant bassoonist let out a cheer and fist-pump. It sent the rest of the orchestra into relieved shouts, and she didn't have the heart to quiet them. They began stamping their feet, the stage vibrating, humming, low and resonant.

Rinna caught her breath, wild possibility flickering through her.

She gestured urgently to the basses. Three of them began to play, finding the note, expanding it. The rest of the section followed, quickly joined by the tubas — bless the tubas. Rinna opened her arms wide, and the string players hastily sat and took up their instruments again.

"D minor!" she cried. "Build it."

The violins nodded, shaping harmonies onto the note. The harpist pulled a trembling arpeggio from her strings, the wind instruments doubled, tripled the sound into an enormous chord buoyed up by breath and bone, tree and ingot, hope and desperation.

The stage pulsing beneath her, she turned to the crowd and waved her arms in wide arcs.

"Sing!" she yelled, though she knew they couldn't hear her.

The word hung in a plume before her. She could just make out the upturned faces below, pale circles in the endless Arctic night.

Slowly, the audience caught on. Sound spread like ripples from the stage, a vast buzzing that resolved into pitch. Rinna raised her arms, and the volume grew, rising up out of five thousand throats, a beautiful, ragged chorus winging into the air.

Beneath their feet, the last of the world's ice began to hum.

The techs looked up from their control room, eyes wide, as high overhead the huge engine spun and creaked.

Rinna tilted her face up, skin stiff as porcelain from the cold, and closed her eyes. She felt it, deep in her bones, a melody singing over and over into the sky. The thrum of sound transformed to super-cooled air, the long hard pull back from the precipice.

Something touched her face, light as feathers, insubstantial as dreams.

Quietly, perfectly, it began to snow.

# JIM TWEEDIE

Jim Tweedie has lived his life in California, Scotland, Utah, Australia, Hawaii, and, most recently, in Long Beach, Washington, across the Columbia River from Astoria, Oregon. He is a pastor, a husband, a father, a grandfather, a poet, a composer, a photographer, a fly fisherman, a beach walker, a teller of stories and, in his spare time, an incurable optimist.

# Something to Sneeze At

This is a story about a sneeze. To understand the sneeze you need to know a few things about the person who sneezed it. His name is Gil.

Gil was born and bred in Ilwaco, Washington, a small fishing town at the mouth of the Columbia River. He had lived there long enough to remember the days when it had been the hub of business and commerce for the entire Long Beach Peninsula. The decline of the salmon industry, the growth of the communities of Long Beach and Ocean Park to the north and, most significant of all, the opening of the Megler Bridge across the Columbia River to Astoria, Oregon, had left the town no less quaint but far less prosperous than it had been back in the day.

Just up the river was the town of Chinook, where folks showed their good humor by wearing sweatshirts with the words, "Chinook — a Small Drinking Town with a Fishing Problem."

In contrast, Gil didn't have a fishing problem and he didn't drink alcohol. His father had done enough of both to convince him at an early age that he would be far better off finding vices of his own. To his surprise, he never found any that appealed to him.

Both then, and later, there was nothing particularly remarkable about Gil. It would be fair and accurate to simply describe him as a good kid who grew up to be a nice guy.

He graduated from the local high school, married, apprenticed as a carpenter (where he acquired the nickname, "Punk"), and raised two daughters who grew up, married and moved away. He retired at 65 years of age and celebrated his 45th wedding anniversary two months before his wife passed away from breast cancer.

It had been a good life but his interest in enjoying more of it had died with his wife and been buried with her in the local cemetery.

After her death, Gil's friends and neighbors tried to get him back on his feet but after hearing him say, "No, thanks," to one invitation after another, they eventually gave it up and left him to himself.

After two years of eating frozen dinners and spending his waking hours staring numbly at the television, Gil woke one morning, stood up, stretched, took a deep breath, and sneezed.

It was not an ordinary sneeze.

To say it was loud would not have done it justice. It was a massive sneeze; a thunderous sneeze; a sneeze that shook the blinds in his bedroom window and sent his dog cowering behind the sofa.

Gil's eyes began to water and his nose began to run like a faucet.

He grabbed a tissue and crawled behind the sofa.

"Now, now, Sophie," he said softly. "It's all right. Poppy just had a sneeze."

As if on cue, his nose began to tingle.

He held his breath, but the tingle grew.

He held his nose, but the sneeze was not to be denied.

"AAA... CHOOOO!"

The blast knocked Gil over like an uprooted Sitka Spruce while Sophie ran to the front door, whining and whimpering as she desperately tried to scratch and claw herself as far away from him as possible.

Gil lay on the floor, listening to Sophie and feeling defeated.

"I'm all right!" he shouted across the room. "Poppy is all right!"

Some master you are, he thought to himself. You bring a dog home from the shelter and five days later, you're already scaring her to death.

Getting Sophie had been Gil's first attempt to start his life over again. He had never owned a dog before so every decision he had to make about dog food, collar, leash, and picking up poop with a plastic bag was a new and exciting adventure. As he had hoped, the house didn't seem quite so empty with Sophie in it and he had even found himself talking to her in the same way he used to talk to...

Gil let the thought pass and grabbed the arm of the sofa. As he pulled himself up, he noted that he needed another tissue.

"What's with the sneezing?" he asked.

He glanced around the room, wondering if his nose had finally succumbed to the two years of accumulated dust.

Gail would have never let things get this out of control, he thought.

He walked over to Sophie, picked her up and cradled her in his arms.

"Now, now, Sophie," he said soothingly. "I promise I won't scare you with a sneeze like that ever again."

Sophie did not look convinced, and Gil immediately regretted the promise when his nose began tingling again.

He set Sophie gently onto the floor and rushed through the front door onto the porch. He somehow managed to close the door behind him before cutting loose with another explosive sneeze.

The sneeze wasn't loud enough to stop a passing car but it was more than enough to stop Gil's neighbor, Potsy, who was walking along the sidewalk in front of Gil's house.

"Terveys, Punk," he yelled in bastardized Finnish.

"Stuff it, Pots," Gil yelled back, using the most refined English idiom he could come up with on the spur of the moment.

It was still early in the day but the mid-summer sun had been up long enough to warm the air and to cause Gil to squint against the glare. His nose was running again, and without a tissue, he did the next best thing as he leaned over the porch railing and drained himself into the long-neglected garden bed below.

Gil may have been a lousy housekeeper but he was an even worse gardener. Before her death, his wife had countered her husband's deficiencies with the touch of a white gloved finger on the furniture and the touch of a green thumb on the plants outside.

Gil looked around the yard and sighed. After two years without weeding or watering, the landscape was as dead and brown as a yard could possibly get in the naturally cool, moist Pacific Northwest.

Where there had once been flowers there were now . . .

Gil paused, marveling at the sight of a massive display of small, scrawny green shrubs with eye-blinding yellow flowers; plants that had sprouted up in seemingly random locations around the yard.

*Cytisus scoparius*, he muttered to himself using the only two botanical Latin words he knew.

Scotch Broom.

The sight of it brought on another sneeze and then another.

He ran back into the house as fast as he could go and slammed the door shut behind him.

"Damn pollen!" he said loud enough to hear himself say it.

So it hadn't been the dust after all.

As his eyes readjusted to the interior darkness of the house he remembered his father's long-ago warning to "Keep away from those devil flowers. If you give 'em a chance, sooner or later they'll kill you for sure!"

Gil's father suffered from constant allergies his entire life and often declared that pollen would finish him off long before alcohol. Each day when he came home from work he'd pour his first shot of whiskey, hold it up, give Gil a wink and say, "It's allergy medicine, boy! Allergy medicine!"

What kind of medicine the second, third and fourth shots were he never bothered to explain.

Scotch Broom was not as widespread back then as it was now. Nowadays it's considered an invasive species, and attempts are made to eradicate it, especially in environmentally sensitive habitats. The seeds can lie in the soil for over 30 years before germinating, which explains why Gil's yard had become infested with the plant.

Ever since they inherited the house from Gil's parents, Gail had spent time each spring carefully pulling the new Scotch Broom shoots from around the house. Now, after being left untouched to grow for over two years, the unplucked sprouts had become large enough to bloom, spread seeds and guarantee their survival for another 30 years.

Gil did some quick calculations and figured that if he systematically pulled the plants out every year he would probably finish them off around the time he turned ninety-seven years old.

"Something to keep me busy," he said to Sophie.

He immediately began creating plans with both short-term and long-term goals. Like a contractor pouring over a blueprint he listed tools and materials he would need and what the final result was going to look like.

When he woke up the next morning, he was surprised to find that he was still sitting at the dining room table. His pencil had dropped to the floor and the paper he had been writing on had become spotted with drippings from his newly dysfunctional sinuses.

He stood up, stretched and started the day off with another sneeze. It was a good sneeze but not on par with the ones that had erupted from his head the day before. Even Sophie took the situation in stride and, perhaps out of sympathy, empathy, or a little bit of both, came through with a small but gratifying sneeze of her own.

"We're a team, aren't we, Sophie?" Gil announced as a smile began to spread across his face. "And like any team, we've got work to do!"

He poured some dry dog food into a bowl for Sophie, freshened her water, and grabbed a stale, half-eaten donut from a reused paper plate on the kitchen counter. While he ate the donut, he changed into his work clothes, scattering crumbs across his bedroom floor as he pulled on his pants.

"It's time for the knight in shining armor to slay the fierce dragon and rescue the fair maiden from her fate-worse-than-death," he proclaimed with an inflection worthy of Monty Python.

He clipped on Sophie's new leash and, side by side, they marched out to the garage. By the time Gil had grabbed a shovel, a pair of clippers and his old carpenter gloves, he was ready to engage the enemy mano a mano in a fight to the death.

His plans called for his first foray to be a sneak attack below the front porch and it wasn't long before he had silently pulled up most of the smaller shoots in the area by the roots. With the small fry out of the way, he lifted the shovel over his head, screamed like a banshee and attacked the largest plants in a furious, frontal assault.

It had been nearly two years since Gil had done heavy-lifting of any kind and digging up just one, deeply-rooted bush left him with barely enough energy to stagger back to the front steps.

So much for Plan A, he sighed. Good thing there's a Plan B.

As it turned out Gil had more plans than the alphabet had letters. He had prepared for every contingency with the same attention to detail that General Patton had shown during the Battle of the Bulge.

Plan B required him to pick up the phone and ask Potsy to come over and help.

Gil was surprised when Potsy said "Yes, I'll be right over." Ten minutes later, he was knocking on Gil's front door armed to the teeth with a chain saw.

After being convinced to trade it in for a shovel, the two neighbors finished up the area around the porch in no time, after which they pressed the attack to the side of the house moving in a clockwise direction. It was like old times for them both.

They enjoyed the day so much that by the time it was over Potsy had invited Gil over for dinner and Gil, without a moment of hesitation, said, "Yes."

It took the two of them three days to get the job done. When they finished, every joint, tendon, ligament and muscle in Gil's body was screaming with pain. The feeling thrilled him. He couldn't remember the last time he had felt so alive.

Through it all Sophie stood nearby, barking encouragement whenever she sensed Gil's enthusiasm was beginning to flag. Just like Gil had said, they had become a team.

Plan B had been a success. The Scotch Broom around his house was gone but the sneezing continued.

Plan C required recruiting his neighbors to rid the entire street of the stuff and Plan D involved petitioning the city council to declare Ilwaco a "Scotch Broom Free Zone".

By the end of the summer Gil had made enough progress on Plan C that he felt ready to put his name on the ballot for city council. He didn't win that year but the following year he was elected and the year after that—the very week he turned seventy years old—he successfully passed an ordinance requiring everyone in Ilwaco to remove Scotch Broom from their property or face a fine.

As it turned out Gil continued to sneeze every day and didn't stop until Sophie died ten years later. The coincidence did not surprise him because long before she died an allergist in Longview told Gil that the pollen in Scotch Broom was too heavy to be an allergen at all. What Gil was allergic to was dog hair.

Gil never mentioned the matter to Sophie but the choice he had to make had been easy. Until the day she died, Gil's every sneeze was a reminder of how important Sophie had become to him.

As for the Scotch Broom, Gil continued to hunt it down until he died at the age of ninety-seven.

As he grew older, Gil often told how his father had been wrong about many things but never so wrong as he had been about Scotch Broom.

"Dad called it a 'devil flower,'" he would say. "But instead of killing me, it gave me a reason to live."

And every time he told the story, he ended it with a sneeze, a wink, and a smile.

# PAM ANDERSON

Pam Anderson has a Master's Degree in TESL and spent most of her teaching career overseas teaching English writing skills in Pakistan, Egypt, Bangladesh, and Indonesia. She accomplished one of her bucket-list goals in 2014 by publishing her memoir and faith journey, *You Are the Needle and I Am the Thread*, which details her adventures and misadventures following her Foreign Service husband while living and working overseas in the Islamic world. Many of the stories in the memoir were previously published in *The Foreign Service Journal*.

The short story, "Heart's Delight," is a chapter taken from an unfinished historical fiction novel set in Afghanistan in the 1980s, which she started writing when she lived in Pakistan. Pam currently teaches a Memoir Writing class at the Lacey Senior Center.

# Heart's Delight

"O Dilkha, what is it?" the mother said as she gently pried the fingers from around the tiny bird, its eyes widened in terror. Her seven-year-old daughter's liquid brown eyes, framed by the sweep of dark lashes, focused on her mother's face and in it her hint of approval as she lifted the tiny creature high for her mother to see. Dilkha, whose name meant heart's delight, was the delight of her mother's life even though she was a girl. She was the last to be born to Rubaba, who though no older than forty-five, was now past her childbearing years. Rubaba's hardscrabble life in the small mountain village in eastern Afghanistan had prematurely aged her, but what value Rubaba lacked in her loss of fertility was more than made up for in the fact that she had produced three strapping sons.

Rubaba's husband, Gul Mohamed, now himself a graybeard, proudly proclaimed, "I have three children and also four daughters." He said the last part somewhat reluctantly, not because he wasn't fond of his daughters, but because like most men of his conservative tribe, he considered his girl children to be merely temporary visitors to his home. They would soon grow up, marry, and then leave his home forever and become part of their husbands' households. The most that one could hope for girl children was for them to marry well, preferably to one's brothers' sons and to produce many sons of their own.

Dilkha's birth, because she was the fourth girl child, was not an occasion to celebrate but to mourn. The village elders came to Gul Mohammed's hujra, the place outside the family's mud-walled home where men congregated to visit, to pay their condolences. Gul Mohammed welcomed his neighbors with the greeting, "My home is poor, but you may sit in the light of my eyes." He motioned his visitors to sit on the threadbare carpet spread out on the bare-swept ground under the portico next to the weathered wooden door.

Sayyid Faridullah, nodding agreement to Gul Mohammed's gracious statement, eased his old bones into the traditional squat, his forearms resting on his knees, and responded kindly, "May God in his mercy give you another son." Sayyid Faridullah's words carried considerable weight in the village because of his title, which signified that he was born into the lineage of the Prophet. Gul Mohammed, eyes downcast, answered with resignation set in the drop of his shoulders, "I am but Allah's servant."

Dilkha was yet another girl to feed and clothe for thirteen or fourteen years until she was of marriageable age. But perhaps she wouldn't live. Infant mortality was high in the desolate tribal lands in this remote area near the mountain border separating Afghanistan from Pakistan, and if a child survived, he was usually of sturdy stock and rarely got sick. Girl children routinely were shortchanged in what was given to them — education, the food they ate after their father and brothers had had their fill, and even medicine when they were sick. Dilkha had come late in life to Rubaba and Gul Mohammed, and maybe it was for this reason that Gul Mohammed consented to the name, Heart's Delight. He fervently believed that all gifts came from God and who was he, Gul Mohammed, a simple man, to question the will of Allah? Therefore, he reluctantly let the tiny bundle squirm her way into his affections.

As Dilkha grew into childhood, she became willful and fearless, a true Afghan. But she was also wide-eyed with curiosity about all living things, and never before had Gul Mohammed seen anyone handle God's creatures with such tenderness and care. She collected a virtual menagerie wherever she went; she followed her older brothers into the fields and found a tiny rabbit; by the irrigation canal she spotted baby turtles lumbering across the sand by the water's edge. She even found a substitute mother for the newborn goat kid whose mother refused to nurse him.

She had the freedom to run and play with the other children after she had finished her chores, and it was this freedom that Dilkha especially cherished. She chafed at the restrictions of the women's life in purdah and unwillingly set herself to the tasks her mother tried to teach her in order that she might grow up to be a good Afghan wife.

Dilkha learned how to tend the fire for the chai, the sweet, milky tea served to visitors as a symbol of hospitality. She learned to mix the flour and water to make naan, the staple food in her village, and to apportion it out properly: one loaf for each adult, one-half for children, and a few thrown into the tandoor (oven) for good measure. She also learned how to treat the bread that she made daily reverently by breaking it, never cutting it with a knife. Like most Afghans, Dilkha's family believed that bread was the first gift God gave Adam after the Fall. The gift of bread signified that God had not deserted mankind after all. Rubaba, ever cognizant of the need to teach Dilkha womanly ways, stressed to Dilkha that the baking of bread was a sacred task and that to have her garments whitened with flour was God's holy work. As Rubaba formed the dough into the paddle shape, she sang one of Dilkha's favorite childhood lullabies:

"Sleep, my darling daughter, sleep!
Today I sing you to sleep…
Sleep, my daughter, sleep…
The light of my life!"

⁓

Dilkha's fingers stumbled over the cloth as she worked her needle in and out of the shalwar kameez she was making for her doll. Her brow knitted in concentration as she fashioned the seams just so as her mother had taught her, and the tip of her tongue protruded from between her lips as she worked hard at the tiny stitches. The outfit she held up for her mother to see was soiled from her dust-grimed hands, but would do.

"Shabash!" Well done! Rubaba smiled at Dilkha as she inspected the little garment. It had taken much effort, but Insha'allah (God willing), Dilkha would learn as her sisters had learned before her, how to become a good wife.

Rubaba's life as an Afghan farmer's wife was a mind-numbing rush of everyday chores, and although she wished a better life for her daughters, she could not foresee any future for her youngest daughter, Dilkha, other than one that mirrored her own. After seven children, Rubaba's arthritic hands were gnarled, her fingers cracked, and their

21

nails almost never clean from tending the vegetable garden, gathering firewood, washing the family's clothes, hauling water for the children's baths, sweeping their mud brick home, wiping children's noses and bottoms, and in her spare time, working on the rug that she was weaving as part of Dilkha's marriage dowry. A resigned sigh escaped from Rubaba's mouth as she foresaw the march of time and a future for Dilkha much like her own.

What troubled Rubaba more than Dilkha's slowness at her womanly tasks, was her headstrong nature. At the age of 10, Dilkha preferred the rough and tumble world of the village boys to the girls' penchant for playing house. What would Dilkha do if the family were unable to find a good match for her? What mother-in-law would accept such an obstinate girl in her home?

"My child, your father and I worry about you so," Rubaba said under her breath, the phrase being a constant refrain that played itself out as incessantly as the sun beat down on the hard-baked soil in their compound.

"But why, Mama?" Dilkha's ears were sharp like those of the hares in the hills. "I don't need a husband. I'm going to become a doctor and help people. You'll see."

"Child, who put such nonsense into your head?" Rubaba snorted in exasperation. Perhaps it had been Aisha, the old dhai, midwife, who tended to the pregnant women and delivered the village babies. Or maybe Dilkha had heard the stories told around the evening fire of the feringhi (foreign) doctors who had saved the life of many a mujahedeen (freedom fighter) unable to make the perilous journey to the Pakistani border on the back of a donkey. At any rate, such nonsense would have to be discarded. No one from their village had ever received enough education to be a doctor — let alone a girl.

As Dilkha neared the age when her time of playing dress-up in her mother's burqa would cease and the donning of the garment that signaled her womanhood would begin, her attention drifted from wild creatures to God's human ones. Her parents acquiesced to this new interest not only because it made Dilkha a more docile child, but also because they recognized in her the talent for healing. The village children flocked to Dilkha with scraped knees and elbows and with the gentle ministrations of her slender fingers, went away soothed and relieved. Her family let her bandage cuts and abrasions and by doing so, contributed to the bank of medicinal information she was slowly building.

It was only natural that Dilkha would be drawn to Aisha, the stooped dhai who served as the villagers' local doctor and pharmacist. Dilkha was soon following Aisha around like a puppy while Aisha tended to the villagers' needs. As Aisha carefully observed her protégée, she was struck by how proficient and diligent a student Dilkha had become in the healing arts. Dilkha spent every waking moment, apart from her required chores at home, studying and committing to memory the medicinal remedies, most taken from common plants, that Aisha used in her doctoring: raisins and walnuts for winter cough; beets for cleansing the liver and increasing menstrual flow; the raw juice of the potato for lessening the pain and stiffness of rheumatism and gout; and the juice of garlic for treating insect bites. These folk remedies and others were passed down through the generations and taken from the Hadith.

Soon the sight of the old, wrinkled crone followed by Dilkha, her figure slight and straight as the letter Alif, became commonplace. To careful observers in the village, it seemed somehow fitting that Dilkha should follow in Aisha's footsteps because Dilkha was growing into a young woman as unconventional as the old woman was.

With much forethought, Aisha had taught Dilkha some rudimentary lessons in how to read and write so that Dilkha wouldn't be totally dependent on her memory to concoct the medicines needed for her future doctoring. Aisha encouraged Dilkha to keep these lessons secret from her family because girls were not supposed to be educated like their brothers. Dilkha delighted in keeping this knowledge hidden, and it served to further shore up her confidence as a girl. I am special because I can read and write like my brothers. Despite knowing the sanctions she would face if their secret ever became public, Dilkha still found it hard to bite her tongue whenever her brothers lorded their superior knowledge over her. She had to remain complicit in her agreement with Aisha.

Aisha and Dilkha worked side by side in the herb and vegetable garden tending the plants with the same care that one devotes to babies. They hoed and plucked out the offensive weeds that threatened to choke the lifeblood from the tender roots. They moved crab fashion among the rows, first tending to the wispy topped carrots and then the broader leafed potatoes. What they couldn't grow themselves, they bought from the village vegetable stall with the few afghanis Aisha had squirreled away as payment for her doctoring. Aisha called to Dilkha across the row of carrots they were pulling, "Child, what do you tell your father about helping me?"

"Oh, Baba doesn't know about us working together, Auntie. I make sure that I delay coming to you until after he's left for his fields in the morning. Mama doesn't mind us working together, but Baba wouldn't think it's proper. He thinks a girl should be home learning from her mother."

Aisha's concentration returned to the carrots she was pulling, but she bit her lip as she considered a plausible explanation for Dilkha's increasingly frequent absences from home while under her tutelage.

Their garden was near the irrigation canal, and they lovingly coaxed the life-giving water into the soil to bring nourishment to the herbs and vegetables. Once the water had gurgled merrily along, giving moisture to each of the fields in the village, but now the water was sluggish. Aisha and Dilkha measured the water each day, fearing the time when it would no longer run. The water level was below the normal low-water mark for autumn.

The village had had water problems before, and once they even had to go to a nearby village closer to the karez to obtain their water. There had always been at least one man they could call upon to fix the underground water system, but now with most of the village men either called on to fight with the mujahedeen against the Russians or graybeards in the village, there was no man young enough to maintain the system. The war against the Soviet infidels had taken not only their young men, but it now threatened to choke off the water that sustained the villagers.

Dilkha's village was lucky in that the war had not come home to them — yet. Sometimes they heard the distant crump of the mortar shells, and at night the sky occasionally lit up like flashes of lightning, but always the sounds of war were distant.

Aisha's hands expertly guided the trowel around the reddish-orange blood carrots and coaxed them out of the ground and into her kameez, which she used apron-fashion. She stood and urged her creaking bones upright as she watched Dilkha bent over the row. Aisha noticed that Dilkha's breasts, which had been like rose buds last year, were now like ripe pomegranates that strained the fabric of her kameez. When Aisha was Dilkha's age, she was already married and heavy with her first child. Aisha decided that she would have to speak to Dilkha's mother. It was also time for Rubaba to let Gul Mohammed know that his daughter was Aisha's understudy. Better for Rubaba to tell him than one of the other villagers who might have noticed all the time Aisha and Dilkha spent together.

"Come, child. We have enough."

"In a minute, Auntie," Dilkha said as she smoothed the hair out of her face with the back of her hand. Dilkha noted the carrots that still needed to be dug, her own large pile and Aisha's rather small one. Aisha's movements seemed to be getting slower with each passing day. Dilkha noted, too, how lined and gray Aisha's face looked lately, almost like the washrags her mother used for cleaning. "I must try to help Auntie more," Dilkha concluded.

Rubaba was waiting at the doorway to their mud-walled home, keeping one eye out for Dilkha's return and the other eye out for Gul Mohammed as he straggled home from the fields. The sun was beginning to dip below the horizon. Rubaba swept her daughter through the door and toward the bucket of water. "Hurry daughter. You need to wash up before your father gets home and help me get the evening meal together." Rubaba nervously scanned the dirt lane for her husband's familiar stooped figure. Finally she spied him in the distance, his head topped by the soiled white turban. Across his shoulder, he carried the wooden-handled hoe, now drooping because of the strain of the day.

"I'm sorry for being late, Mama, but I had to stay and help Auntie. She's getting so tired, and she needs help harvesting the vegetables and herbs from our garden."

"Shh. You can tell me later. Help me get the rice and vegetables on the table."

Rubaba and Dilkha formed a united front as they ushered Gul Mohammed into the house and motioned him toward the bucket of wash water. Rubaba took the hoe from her husband's dirt-grimed hands and placed it outside the door, propped up against the mud wall.

"You'll never believe what the men were talking about in the tea stall at lunch time."

"What was it?" Rubaba asked.

"The old dhai — it seems like she has a young girl who is learning her doctoring ways."

"Oh, yes?" Rubaba said, somewhat warily.

"All the men are wagging their tongues, but they don't know who the young girl is. Apparently they saw the two of them working in Aisha's vegetable garden — from a distance. You know it's all right for the girl to help Aisha in her garden, but I hope Aisha doesn't take it any farther. She's only in the position she's in because she's the widow of the old hakim, Amin. "

Dilkha offered brightly, "But Baba, Aisha is the only person in the village who can help the villagers with their ailments. There's no one else. What's wrong with her teaching someone to take her place?"

"My child, it's just not done!" Gul Mohammed thundered. "It's not a woman's role to be doctoring other than helping women birth their babies. She's going against our traditions. When you start breaking traditions, the whole of village life breaks down. What next? Women working as tailors? Women teaching school?" Gul Mohammed's wiry steel gray eyebrows threatened to meet in the center of his wrinkled, sun scorched brow.

Dilkha's bright eyes met his in a defiant gaze, but after a few long moments, she cast her eyes downward. Dilkha had been trained from early childhood to be submissive, but her training fought her nature as she inwardly railed at the traditions which kept women housebound and ignorant. Surely her hidebound father could see that the village needed the skills of both men and women, especially now during times of war.

The next day, Dilkha came early to Aisha's house to help with the making of the carrot halwa, the sweet pudding made with carrots, sugar, and milk. Instead of Aisha's usual cheery greeting, her wan voice called out, "May God's peace and blessings be upon thee, child."

Dilkha approached the tired form on the charpoy, the rope bed, and replied, "May faith be thy daily bread," but immediately she wished she had used some other form of greeting, for Aisha's face was the picture of weariness.

26

Aisha opened her eyes and held out her hand to Dilkha. "Come sit," she said with great effort. The rope around the wooden-framed charpoy creaked as Dilkha perched on the edge of the bed and smoothed Aisha's wrinkled brow. She clasped Aisha's work-worn hands in hers and said, "You must take something to drink and eat." Dilkha's eyes traveled to Aisha's parchment papery skin that hung loosely on her arms and hands.

"No, I cannot. The smell of food turns my stomach."

"But you must have something."

"Promise me you'll take care of the villagers when I'm gone. We need to let your father know now while there's still time for him to get used to the idea."

"Of course I will, Auntie, but don't talk of that now. When you are better, Insha'allah, we shall work side-by-side as we have always done."

Dilkha busied herself fetching water and boiling it over the fire to make tea for Aisha. She returned to Aisha's bedside and gently lifted her head so she could take some of the liquid. Dilkha carefully wiped away the drops that escaped from Aisha's drawn lips. "Where does it hurt, Auntie?"

"My muscles ache so," Aisha replied, pointing to the whole of her body.

Dilkha lifted the sheet to smooth it and noticed the dark, rice-water stool staining the bedclothes. The words slipped from her mouth with a quick intake of air as she recognized the unmistakable dead mouse smell of cholera that permeated the bedclothes. "Oh, Auntie, you have taken the sickness!" The whites of Aisha's eyes had taken on a strange cast, contrasting sharply with the salt-and-pepper hair hung limply over the pillow in a braid.

Dilkha quickly went to the shelf, cracked an egg into a bowl, and separated the white from the yellow. With her fingers she smeared the raw egg white on Aisha's face and head. She didn't have a chicken skin to tie around Aisha's body, so the egg white would have to do. "I will stay and help you," Dilkha said as she smoothed the white into her Auntie's crinkly skin.

Aisha sensed the fear in Dilkha's voice but felt only stillness in her own heart. "Be calm, my child. It is only Allah's way of taking away the sins I have committed."

The hours passed quickly, but it seemed like each one dragged on in worry as Dilkha was consumed with her nursing chores. She forced the tea between Aisha's lips several times a day in an effort to keep the liquid in her body, but she was unable to get Aisha to eat, not even a small piece of naan. Dilkha cleansed Aisha's body with sponge baths and disposed of the soiled linens in the fire so that the sickness would not spread to the others.

As nighttime approached, the village women came to take over nursing Aisha so Dilkha could get some rest. The other women recognized the course of the sickness and its inevitable outcome, but Dilkha was not experienced enough in caring for old people to know when their reserves of strength were exhausted. Perhaps her love for Aisha also prevented her from facing the truth.

The next day Aisha grew weaker until at last her diarrheal output exceeded the liquid that Dilkha forced between Aisha's lips. The skin on Aisha's arms formed a tent when pinched, and her eyes took on a vacant, unblinking look. Aisha's breathing became shallow, and she gradually drifted into a coma, unable to respond to Dilkha's tearful pleas.

"Dear Auntie, don't leave me," Dilkha cried as she clung to Aisha's hands, which seemed so cold, the skin on the back of her hands parchment thin and covered with blue tracings of veins. Dilkha, exhausted by her nursing, sat by the edge of the charpoy and slumped over into a deep sleep.

The end, although expected, crept in silently leaving Dilkha unaware. She woke with a start and noticing Aisha's deathlike pallor, placed her ear over the old woman's heart to listen for the faint beating, but she could hear nothing. She closed Aisha's eyelids and wiped the tears from her own. "Khuda hafiz, go with God," she whispered. Aisha was gone.

Rubaba came to Aisha's place to usher Dilkha home so the village women could tend to Aisha's body. They washed her body and carefully wrapped a shroud of muslin around her. Beneath her chin and around her head, a cloth was tied to prevent her jaw from gaping open.

Because Aisha had no surviving sons, four men from the village were chosen as pallbearers. They gently placed Aisha's white-shrouded body on a charpoy and carried it towards the cemetery. The other village men and boys followed behind, forming the funeral cortege. Only the women were left behind to mourn privately.

After the grave was dug and Aisha's body eased into it, the village mullah recited verses from the Qur'an and ended the ceremony with a poem by the 17th-century Pathan poet, Abd-ur Rahman:

> ... So fast our friends depart unto the grave,
> As the caravan with speed returneth home,
> So very promptly doth death deal with us,
> As the reaper cutteth down the ripe corn.

The thud of the dry earth clods on the shroud-covered body signaled an end to Aisha's life. Although separated by custom from taking part in the funeral, Dilkha felt the earth clods reverberate in her heart; it left her with a mournful coldness that made her wonder if she was feeling the passing of Aisha's soul from her body.

Those mourning at the gravesite felt no such connection to the dead, but they took comfort in the knowledge that Aisha was now with her Maker in Paradise.

—

Aisha was not the only villager felled by cholera. The disease spread like wildfire from family to family, taking equally the elderly and the very young. Although Dilkha was mindful of the required period of mourning after Aisha's death, she had no time for it because of the need to respond to the villagers' pleas for help. Dilkha would now become the bulwark in the villagers' fight against the disease, and she scurried from house to house in her attempt to stem the epidemic.

Rubaba knew that the baton had been passed between Aisha and her daughter. It was now time to inform Dilkha's father. Rubaba waited until the house had hushed from the busy day and they were tucked into bed. "Husband, do you remember when you told me about the villagers' gossip concerning Aisha and her young understudy?"

Gul Mohammed turned over in bed to face Rubaba, even though her form was but an outline in the dark. "Yes, what of it?"

Rubaba hesitated only slightly, "It's time you knew that the young girl is our daughter." Rubaba heard Gul Mohammed sputter in his consternation. "Before you get upset, may I remind you that you have watched our daughter grow into a young woman with skills befitting her age. She may not have the cooking and housekeeping skills of other girls, but those she has are far better. Aisha passed her knowledge of traditional herbal medicine on to our daughter," Rubaba noted with pride. "Remember, these are the medicines that appear in our Hadith. How could this be wrong?"

"But doctoring is a man's job. What will others say?"

"They will say that with Aisha's passing, Dilkha is the only one in the village standing between us and death. There is no hakim within three days' walking distance. There are no young men left in the village to study the hakim's ways. They've all been called to fight the war. Who else is there?"

As Gul Mohammed considered this revelation, he felt conflicted, like a piece of naan torn in two, between his pride as the head of a traditional household, keeping a tight rein over his womenfolk and the equal pride he felt toward his daughter as the savior of the village. What is a simple man like me to do? What a dilemma to be facing at my age in these difficult times.

"Please tell me you'll allow our Dilkha to continue. Don't dismiss her out of hand. Tell me you'll pray to Allah about this and ask for His wisdom."

Gul Mohammed tossed and turned through the night like the soil that is upended by the blade of the plow as it furrows the soil. He wracked his brain to think of some way out of the predicament. What precedent could he point to in order to convince his fellow villagers? Wasn't the wife of the Prophet Mohammed a businesswoman? Didn't the Prophet consult his wife on matters of importance? But my Dilkha is no prophetess. But these are harsh times with many dead from this illness. The air reeks from the fires that burn the soiled linens.

Gul Mohammed kept vigil along with the cock as it waited for dawn to announce the new day. Finally, he rose from his bed and announced to his also wakeful wife, "All right. She has my permission to continue her doctoring."

Rubaba's heart soared as she slid out of bed to wake Dilkha with the good news. Dilkha greeted Gul Mohammed's decision with exhausted relief, but there was no time to tarry. As Dilkha continued nursing the villagers with cholera, she compiled a bank of answers to her endless questions among those afflicted: How many family members are sick? When did the illness come on? When did you last eat? What did you eat? How did you wash the vegetables? Where did you draw your water? Did you boil it? Did you wash your hands before preparing your children's food?

Although many villagers saw Dilkha as a lifesaver, others did not, and village gossip was rampant. Dilkha was often the subject of the elders' scorn in the chaikhana, the village tea stall that was known as the local "newspaper made of bricks." It was here where the men congregated to discuss the price of their crops while sipping their tea. It was here also where Gul Mohammed chafed under his friends' censure, despite no one's outward condemnation of Dilkha's conduct. Gul Mohammed read his friends' displeasure on their faces and felt shame and pride battle within him. Which would win out?

He returned late one evening to find Rubaba sitting by the dim light of the hearth mending one of his shalwar kurtas, torn by the brambles in the field. He interrupted her concentration with a forceful whisper, "This has to stop!" He did not wish to wake his daughter, who had fallen into an exhausted but fitful sleep on the charpoy in the shadows of the room. He could see her cracked and chapped hands pillowed under her head. The images of her constantly washing, washing her hands flitted through his mind.

Rubaba looked up from her sewing and asked, "Who's been talking?"

Gul Mohammed replied, "No one outwardly, but I can see it in their faces when they avert their eyes and condemn me because I can't control my own daughter."

After a moment of careful consideration, Rubaba said, "What's more important to you, your standing in the village or your daughter's happiness? Don't you see the good work she's been doing, the lives she's saved?"

Gul Mohammed, still focused on his own feelings, barely heard Rubaba's questions. "Sayyid Faridullah is the worst of the lot — more so than the other men in judging me."

Rubaba, her head bent over her mending, cut the thread with her teeth and looked up at Gul Mohammed standing beside her, his brows knitted together in frustration at the situation he found himself in. "I'll bet that the great Sayyid didn't tell you that Dilkha saved the life of his grandson, little Aminullah, did he?" Rubaba said with no little sarcasm. "Did he tell you how she nursed the little one late into the night?" Rubaba's brain was searching for evidence to compile and present. "Was Faisal at the chaikhana? Did he tell you that Dilkha has been teaching the village women to boil their water and wash their hands with soap before preparing food? Did Faisal mention that our daughter saved his wife's life, that without Dilkha his children would have been left without a mother?" She paused as she gave time for her words to penetrate her husband's shell of protection that he had built around him like armor. "What about Haji Suleiman? He was left in such a weakened state that he couldn't work his field."

The torrent of words spilled out of Rubaba's mouth as she presented example after example of Dilkha's work among the villagers. In the case of the men who had fallen ill to cholera, Rubaba reminded Gul Mohammed that Dilkha followed the strict guidelines against nursing the men directly. Instead, she instructed their womenfolk in how to keep their men hydrated by giving them either sweet or salted lemon juice in an effort to keep fluids in their bodies and to ease the discomfort in their bowels. Dilkha also taught them how to make a concoction from the root of the guava tree in boiled water to prevent the nausea and vomiting that accompanied cholera. All these remedies Dilkha had learned as Aisha's understudy.

Rubaba urged her husband to speak to the village council, to advocate on their daughter's behalf. "Speak to them tomorrow before the rumors about Dilkha spread. Tell them about all the things she has implemented in the village — improved cleanliness and proper latrines; being the first to see the connection between the broken karez and the outbreak of cholera; teaching the mothers about the importance of boiling their water. She has worked so hard..." Rubaba's words trailed off. She could see Gul Mohammed's internal debate between his love for his daughter and his equal desire to maintain the respect of the village elders.

After several moments, Gul Mohammed sighed and said, "I'll speak with them." His mind tried to formulate how he would counter their claims of wrongdoing with evidence of how Dilkha had single-handedly helped the villagers change their minds and hearts concerning their health habits and slowed the course of the epidemic.

Early the next morning as the pearly dawn penetrated the shadows that still lingered from the night, Gul Mohammed trod the path to the mud-walled community center in the middle of the village, where the village council met. As he walked, his feet left small clouds of dust in his wake, which clung stubbornly to his farmer's leather chappals.

Arriving at the center, his hand grasped the wrought-iron door handle, which was fastened to the wooden door, which was hung slightly askew in the door frame of the mud structure. Gul Mohammed noticed that the mud walls held their imprint of the countless hands that had shaped and smoothed the building's surface, patting here and there, evidence of the myriad hands involved in the construction of this communal meeting place. The imprint of his hands was among those handprints. New mud had been applied to the walls to hide the surface cracks in them, cracks that appeared as the walls battled the ravages of spring rain, summer heat, and cold winters. The building resembled the other village buildings — flat-roofed and rather plain in its dun color, but this building was mute, unlike the village homes, where one heard children's voices. This building gave no hint of the importance of the proceedings soon to be contained within.

He leaned toward the door, his gnarled hands grasping the handle firmly, and he pushed hard to overcome the resistance of the door's initial opening. He heard the customary squeak of hinges that needed oiling. He swallowed the phlegm that had gathered at the back of his throat, squared his shoulders, and wondered whether this day's outcome would be any different than other outcomes that had emanated from this council's deliberations.

Gul Mohammed had worn his best shalwar kurta, his newest one, the one without telltale signs of mending, the one he kept for special occasions such as this. Gul Mohammed's mind settled briefly on the memory of his Rubaba, who had lovingly washed his outfit and had ironed it with the heavy iron, which she had heated over the fire, only the night before. The cuffs of his kurta hid the burly knobs of his wrists — good, strong, farmer's wrists, thickened with much use. Around his head he wore the usual white turban, the coils of fabric wound just so. His beard and mustache were neatly trimmed, befitting this important occasion.

Gul Mohammed's bearing was erect and his gaze was steadfast as he stood and resolutely faced the august council seated before him. Nearest the door sat Sayyid Faridullah, the head of the council, who bade Gul Mohammed to sit. Gul Mohammed's eyes swept from one elder to the next as he contemplated which of them might be his supporters and which his adversaries.

There was Feroz, seated at the far end of the circle of men sitting cross-legged on the rug, its pattern of elephant's foot, mostly obscured by the men seated upon them. Feroz was among Gul Mohammed's oldest friends, the friend of his youth, and as Feroz looked at him in a kindly and sympathetic manner, the spirits of Gul Mohammed lifted. "Good morning," Feroz offered, breaking the silence of the phalanx of elders.

Gul Mohammed replied warmly, "Good morning, my friend."

Next to Feroz sat Akbar, mouth set firmly. Akbar's eyes gazed beyond him, through him, to the wall behind him, perhaps in an effort to ignore the person brought before the council. Gul Mohammed tried to determine whether that firmness of mouth and unwillingness to meet him in the eye represented disdain for himself, his Dilkha, or perhaps a mind already made up. Akbar would most likely not be an advocate.

Hamid looked noncommittal, but Gul Mohammed knew Hamid to be a weak man, easily swayed by the opinions of others. Hamid sat next to Akbar and conversed quietly, eyes never departing from Akbar's visage. Perhaps Hamid was trying to curry favor from his opinionated neighbor.

Gul Mohammed fixed his eyes on the last of the five-member council. Ahmed sat ramrod straight, his fingers tracing the elephant's foot pattern in the carpet near his feet, first forward then backward. Like the other graybeards, Ahmed was attired in the traditional shalwar kurta and turban, but he also wore an embroidered vest, an indication of his relative wealth in the village. Ahmed's fingers were not those of a farmer but a merchant. Ahmed was the village grocer, whose small store stocked the staples in the village: flour, oil, rice, and tea. Gul Mohammed watched as Ahmed's fingers traced the warp and woof of the carpet's design, back and forth, back and forth, and Gul Mohammed thought that perhaps the tracings represented the vagaries of Ahmed's mind as he mulled the pros and cons of the dilemma before them. Would Ahmed favor Dilkha and her work or would he stick to the conventional ways of the village?

Gul Mohammed had rehearsed his speech in his mind endlessly, and he hoped that Allah would give wings to his words so they would pierce the hearts of the esteemed elders arrayed before him. He cleared his throat as he began. "Do you remember these many years ago when my youngest daughter was born? The evening began auspiciously when my wife's pains started on the eve of our Prophet's birthday. All night and all the next day I waited for the good news of my next son's birth. My wife's pains and her screams kept increasing, and I despaired that I would lose either my wife or my son, or perhaps both."

"Aisha had given Rubaba an infusion of black seed (Nigella seed) boiled in water with honey, but it seemed of no avail, and the pains continued. Finally, the old dhai summoned me with the news that a child was born to me, and it was a daughter, not a son. As you remember, my disappointment was great." Gul Mohammed's face softened as he remembered seeing his last born for the first time.

He peered at Sayyid Faridullah as he emphasized his next words. "Do you remember how you consoled me, my friend, and told me that you had hoped God would bless me with another son? Despite your wish, Allah didn't. Instead, he gave me a daughter. I had prayed fervently for a son, but Allah, in his wisdom, granted me a daughter. Who was I to question the will of Allah? Perhaps He had a plan for this child, this child born of our old age." Gul Mohammed's mind traveled back in time to the first look he had of his tiny daughter, a gift from God, a precious life that had been entrusted to his care. She was fair and rosy with long dark lashes and arched brows. Her hands and feet were delicate — she was perfect in every way. "As I looked at my daughter's beautiful face, I felt I had found God."

Gul Mohammed expressed his unabashed love for his daughter in the following words. "My friends, I believe that my Dilkha was a gift from God. She has tried my patience along with yours through these many years, but I believe she was given to us for a purpose, maybe for this very crisis we face today. Who other than Dilkha has been able to step in and fill the void after the old dhai's death?" Gul Mohammed searched the line of old, wrinkled faces, and his gaze fixated on the rheumy eyes before him. "If you can find any gratitude in your hearts for what my daughter has done for your families and for our village, I pray that you would have mercy on her and on me, an old man who just wants what's best for his daughter." He waited in hushed silence as his fellow graybeards debated among themselves.

All of the council had family members who had fallen ill. Their wives had talked about Dilkha's training in water and healthy habits, and most of the men had witnessed Dilkha's late-night vigils by the bedside of their sick children or grandchildren. It seemed somehow hypocritical to acknowledge their debt to this young woman and at the same time deny her opportunity to continue working. But yet… her work in the village was highly irregular… no one so young had been allowed before, especially a girl. Tongues wagged and words flew back and forth as the men pondered Dilkha's future and, possibly, the fate of their village.

Finally, Sayyid Faridullah rose from his seat and proclaimed, "As elders, we are responsible for the decisions affecting the health and safety of the villagers entrusted to our care. On the one hand, your daughter has been working despite our consent in the matter. This is inexcusable. We had allowed the old dhai to work only because of the respect we all felt for her late husband, our esteemed hakim."

"On the other hand, we must acknowledge the lives she has saved and the changes she has wrought in our village, perhaps changes for the better. But both you and I know that our lives are governed by the words of our great Prophet, and his words cannot be treated lightly. We have lived by these words for centuries, and they have served us well. What would happen if we threw aside convention and conformed to the ways of this world? We would be no better than the infidels that we fight." Sayyid paused for emphasis, "No my friends, we must cling to our ways, our old, trusted ways. We all know that Allah sends illness to some and not others to teach them the error of their ways. Perhaps we've offended Him in some way, and He's merely eliminating the sins from our souls. The old ways are best, you must agree." Sayyid Faridullah nodded toward the door, indicating that Gul Mohammed's time was up and that there was no recourse. His concluding words and his cold demeanor seemed as harsh and unbending as the callus on his forehead, a mark of a pious man who had repeatedly prostrated himself in prayer.

Gul Mohammed's heart sank as Sayyid Faridullah's pronouncement penetrated his skull. He managed a polite farewell, but the words betrayed his facial features, which refused to conform to the words. He walked resolutely toward the door, eager to be alone with his thoughts. What will I tell my Dilkha? What's to become of us if she is not allowed to help the villagers? Can I go against the will of the council? How can I convince them? My daughter will be devastated...

Dilkha and Rubaba waited in the doorway of their home, eager to hear the council's decision. They fidgeted with their head coverings, fingering the fabric again and again. Dilkha was the first to glimpse Gul Mohammed's dejected frame, his feet scudding against the dirt path.

"Oh, no. It can't be," Dilkha whispered under her breath. Tears began to flow from her eyes, and her chin trembled at the finality of the decision even before she heard the words from her father's lips.

Rubaba drew her daughter to her shoulder, her own tears flowing like a stream.

Gul Mohammed pulled his daughter and his wife into his embrace and uttered soothing words. "Shh, now. We'll get through this. We'll fight this together somehow. They'll change their minds... they have to." He put his hands on Dilkha's shoulders and drew his face close to hers so he could look into the puddles that obscured her eyes. "Oh, my daughter, what pains you, pains me. This isn't the end of things. The illness goes on, and all it takes is for one of the council to be stricken himself. Then he'll come to you on bended knee asking for help."

"Oh, Baba. How can you be so sure?" Dilkha choked out the words between sobs.

Gul Mohammed took his massive, callused thumbs and gently wiped the runnels of Dilkha's tears. He searched her eyes. "I don't know anything for sure other than this: your mother named you Dilkha because you were the delight of our hearts so late in life. As you've grown into a young woman, I've seen your heart's delight fulfilled in your work — your doctoring. Allah has sent you to us for a reason, and I believe He wants you to live out His plan for you, and in doing so, become the delight of His heart." Gul Mohammed's eyes misted over, but there was a smile on his face as he consoled his daughter. He placed his rough farmer's hands on each side of Dilkha's face and leaned closer so that their noses were almost touching. "So, no more tears. According to His will, your heart's desire will come to pass."

# Keith Eisner

Keith Eisner lives in Olympia, where
he writes, teaches creative writing
at the Olympia Senior Center, acts
in local productions, and listens to
baseball on the radio. He thanks the
TRL staff for their hard work and
dedication in producing this anthology
that celebrates local writers — may
we have many more! He dedicates his
story to his mother, Janet Ruth Lackey.

# Christmas, 1957

On the first weekend after Pearl Harbor Day, the merchants in our part
of Detroit strung lights on all the lampposts along Woodward Avenue.
When night fell, we'd climb into the old brown De Soto and go for a
ride down the avenue. My sisters and I would kneel on the back seat
and gaze out the rear window at the transformed town. Red, green,
blue and red again — the lights from one post merged into the next.
When we closed our eyes half-shut, there was a wall of color. When we
went faster, the gaps of black shrank to pencil lines. My Christmases
come out of that wall of light and darkness. One blends into the next
and I have to open my eyes and look sharp to make out the particular
shape of one Christmas from another. I look now and see the colors of
the reindeer cookies on the kitchen table…

There's a small yellow kitchen at the back of an apartment. Generally,
it's a plain, often cold room, but today it's full of warmth, good smells
and Christmas music. Three children sit at the table with doughy
fingers and flour on their clothes. They look up often with wonder and
delight at the woman in the center of the room. For there is the feeling
that the warmth and good smells are not coming from the old white
stove; that the rousing music is not coming from the radio on top of
the refrigerator, but that all this is coming from her.

Since early morning, she's been orchestrating the Christmas baking
and decorating. There are cut-out butter cookies of bells and angels,
snowmen and Santas. Every bowl in the house is in use. Even our plain
old cereal bowls have been transformed into vessels of color, each
bearing a different shade of frosting. She rolls out more dough for us
and reminds my little sister to dip the cutter in flour first so the dough
won't stick. It sticks anyway. We press down so hard that dough oozes
through the tiny holes in the top of the cutter. Then we like to gently
lift the cookie cutter and watch the figure of a reindeer or an angel

peel out slowly onto the table. There are no fights today. We have been borne along on a river of warmth and light. We sing: *Good King Wenceslas looked out on the Feast of Stephen when the snow lay round about, deep and crisp and even.*

The big moment of the day comes when a special batch of reindeer cookies have cooled. These are for school. I was afraid to volunteer to bring cookies for Christmas week because of my stepfather's grumbling about making more work for my mother. She works during the days and sometimes on nights and weekends, and I miss her deeply. But when I asked about the cookies, she brightened and dismissed out of hand my stepfather's comment that we just pick up a bag of Oreos.

The table is cleared now except for the reindeer and the flanking bowls of icing. She fills the cake decorator — a gift from last Christmas with 18 attachments — and gives each reindeer a chocolate brown body, tan antlers, a white tail, black hooves and a blazing red nose. At school, the classroom is amazed. Even my worst enemy, Elmer Gantner, is silenced, and my best friend, Nabil Hazamy, says right out loud: *You must have the best mother in the whole world!* The class laughs; a good, rare laugh with no teasing or mockery.

Later that day Nabil, Joe Chilean and I work on our paper chain. For the past week, we've been making it during free time, carefully coiling it in a box as our plan is to take it out the last school day and astound everyone with its length and beauty. But today when I look up, I see Elmer and Jimmy Edwards sauntering over to us. I groan. Jimmy is the class bully and Elmer is his jackal.

"Hey, Blanchard," Jimmy says to me, "watcha doing?" There's no mistaking the menace in his voice, and no one can beat him. However the only guy Jimmy can't beat, the only kid who's fought him to a standstill every time is fearless little Joe Chilean, who says, "What's it to you, Edwards?"

Jimmy's reply is a sliding step forward and a kick of our box — a calculated tap not hard enough to do any damage, but too much to ignore. Joe drops his scissors and stands. His chair clatters on the floor behind him, and I can see what's going to happen. They'll jockey around the box, making threats and counter-threats until Jimmy shoves him (Joe never attacks first) and then they'll be rolling around on the floor, scattering desks and chairs and punching each other ferociously. Mrs. Wallace will come over with her ruler, and a scream from one of the girls will bring Mr. Harrison from across the hall to break it up. The chain will be gone then. Even if it somehow escapes being crumpled and torn during the fight, its spirit will be snapped. Our bustling energy will be replaced by a flat hostility. I see each scene unfold before Joe's chair hits the floor and wait unhappily for its occurrence.

But Nabil surprises us all. "Hey," he asks, "you guys want to help?" Without a second of hesitation or a flicker of acknowledgment of the code he's breaking, he steps between the two fighters and, turning over the box, gently shakes our secret out onto the floor. "Look at this!" he says, kneeling beside the small mountain and holding up handfuls of paper chain. We stare. He doesn't wait for a reply. "Elmer, why don't you get your scissors and that gold paper you showed me yesterday — you still got it?"

Elmer, who has had his mouth open (as I'm sure I have), looks once to Jimmy, who is not looking at him, then turns and goes to his desk. Jimmy looks warily at us. His knuckles whiten, then relax and whiten again. Nabil ignores this and goes on chattering, asking Jimmy to bring over his stapler, volunteering my staples, and uncoiling the chain like a hypnotizer with a sleeping snake. Joe smiles, picks up his chair and sits down. Finally Jimmy shrugs, goes to his desk and returns with his stapler.

Other kids are watching us now and Nabil waves them over, giving directions about scissors, paper and tape until the whole class is involved. Mrs. Wallace hesitates, but recognizing an irresistible force when she sees one, cancels geography and extends free time for the rest of the afternoon. She steps into her storeroom and brings out reams of construction paper. We push the chairs back to the wall and work on the floor.

Nabil is not still for a second. He organizes and re-organizes the groups of chain-makers, collects the chains and adds them to the end of the big chain in the middle of the floor. Mrs. Wallace puts on a Christmas record, and before the first carol is over the chain is long enough to go across the room twice. I cannot recall when I have ever felt the class this happy and purposeful. But the energy has not peaked

41

yet. Nabil remembers that some girls in Mr. Harrison's class have also been making a chain, and wouldn't it be great if... With Mrs. Wallace's permission, he goes to ask.

Elmer asks Mrs. Wallace if we can use her paper-cutter. She pauses, then says, "Yes, if you're extremely careful." She tells him to pick a helper. To my surprise, he doesn't pick Jimmy Edwards or Joe Chilean, but me. We're quiet at first — he cutting and I feeding him the paper — and shy; shy at the sudden intimacy of enemies. I look at him as he concentrates on the cutting: the paleness of his face, the squarish jaw, the strand of blond hair over his deep-set eyes, the thin bluish vein across his temple. He came from down South a year ago with just his mother and little sisters. He's not good at sports and terrible at schoolwork. I see him hanging around with different kids, but I don't know if he really has any friends at school. Maybe Jimmy is his friend and maybe not. I don't know why we're enemies any more than I know why Nabil and I are friends. It just happens that way. I never knew what to say to Elmer even before we became enemies and I don't know what to say to him now.

But he begins to talk. "I may be going down home this week," he says and tells me that he and his mother and sisters, if they can get the money from his grandpa, will take the train home for Christmas. His grandpa has chickens and a big black dog in his yard, and they'll be eating fresh cured ham and bacon. He tells me about his grandpa and his uncles—all mighty, rifle-toting men. "Up here, people all talk about *hillbillies*, but they don't know. My grandpa, he's the real thing. Sure, he's ignorant like the ones on TV about city ways and stuff, but he ain't no fool."

My picture of the South is a balmy place where watermelons and cotton grow year round. So when I ask him what Christmas is like being so hot and without snow — do they go swimming? — he laughs. It's way too cold for swimming, he tells me, but they don't get snow. Often on Christmas mornings, though, there's a hard frost all around and you can see tracks of raccoon and deer. There's a pretty, little river behind his grandpa's and a lot of the river rocks on the banks are covered with ice, and they go looking for the brightest ones with "pie-rite — that's fool's gold" in them. Looking at the blade cutting the paper so evenly, he's back there now, and for a moment, I too can see a train full of Southerners going home and can hear the river running through ice. "Maybe," he says, "I can bring you one of them rocks. Course the ice'll be melted by then, but they're still pretty." I tell him I'd like that.

Nabil has gotten Mr. Harrison's class involved and the chain stretches between the two classrooms. The goal is as obvious as a mountain summit: to make a paper chain long enough to reach from one end of the hall to the other before the 3:30 bell rings in less than an hour. Nabil is at fever pitch now, supervising the making, moving and consolidation of the chains. Kids run between the rooms, bearing loops of chain. Elmer and I are quiet again, working twice as fast to keep everyone supplied. Mr. Harrison and Mrs. Wallace sit at her desk, drinking coffee and watching. The steam radiator comes on, banging and clanking away under the windows. Mrs. Wallace turns up her phonograph. I hear it say: *from angels bending near the earth to touch their harps of gold.*

The chain is finished a good 15 minutes before the bell rings. Without stretching it tight, 42 kids hold a chain of red, green, yellow, white, blue and purple construction paper. At one end of the hall, Theodore Little thumbtacks an end of the chain to the wall above the fire-escape door. Nabil stands on a chair in the center of the hall, holding a length of golden paper chain high above his head. At the other end of the hall, standing in the open doorway with snowflakes all around, is my friend Elmer holding the end of the chain in both hands.

—

It's here every year: memory. It's somewhere just behind the lights, weaving in and out of the loops and links of paper chain. A piece of tinsel, like a strand of silver hair, falls from the top of the tree with no sound... and with almost no time either. It's lovely as it drifts through regions of light and shadow.

Elmer never did bring me that rock, and in January for reasons as inexplicable as his choosing me to help with the paper-cutter, we were enemies again. But the memory remains. The child in the doorway remains and grows stronger while the rest fades into the black outlines.

Meagan Macvie grew up in Alaska writing poems about injustice and hot boys. After studying poetry and literature at the University of Idaho, she spent fifteen years in government communications before breaking up with her career to again pursue creative writing. In 2014, she received her MFA in fiction from Pacific Lutheran University. She is currently seeking agent representation for her first novel and is working on a second. Her writing has appeared in *Narrative*, *Fugue* and *The Anchorage Press*. She lives in Littlerock, Washington with her husband, daughter, cat, dog, and fourteen chickens. She is grateful to her family and friends for their support, and most especially to her fellow writers — both peers and mentors — who continue to inspire, encourage and challenge her.

# Going Without

Gracie barely speaks these days. Not that my nine-year-old was a big talker before the accident, but lately she's gone mute.

Take this morning. We're driving to soccer practice and she's in the back, belted into our Volvo's middle seat — the safest — and I say, "Today's the big BBQ."

Gracie shrugs as she watches the neighborhood houses slide by her window.

"You're practicing at the field nearest the lake," I say, "the one with the fence along the back … and after, swimming!"

She nods, her eyes still glued to the window.

Gracie loves swimming. She's our Little Fish. Barry took her to Mommy-and-Me before she was even walking. He was the only daddy in the class. You'd think he cured cancer the way those moms praised him each week for how patient he was with Gracie, how encouraging. She was a natural, though, so it didn't take much. She swam on her own by the second class. Barry proudly hung her Baby Nemo award on his home office wall between his professional engineer license and his "Plan. Prepare. Perform." poster.

I started Gracie in KinderSwim when she was five. She's been with the Tidal Waves — an accredited USA swimming club — ever since. She's got an amazing breaststroke, and wins most of her races. I can't wait for her to start competing on senior team. That's where she'll make her mark. Right now, she's just having fun — she's a kid — but I tell her if she keeps up, keeps working hard and improving her strokes, she'll be elite someday. Maybe go on to the Olympics.

My skin's already sticky, even with the AC blasting. I lean my face into the cool airstream angled toward the backseat. My shoulder jostles her too-tall aluminum water bottle, but I manage to grab it before the canister topples from my cup holder. I hold it up so Gracie can see her brown, BPA-free Klean Kanteen covered in orange and yellow owls. "Brought your lucky one! Can't have my favorite girl getting dehydrated." Ice cubes clink as the sweating bottle tips back and forth. My fingers lose their grip. The bottle skids across the passenger seat, ricochets off the door, and lands on the gray floor mat. "Oh, Grace. Your mom is such a klutz!"

I want to grab for the bottle, wipe the dark wet mark off the passenger seat, but I'm driving on the freeway and there's no way I'm risking my daughter's life. Anyway, the Volvo's leather seats are no strangers to spills; a little water won't matter.

Not even eleven and already the dash thermometer reads eighty-nine. My back is sweating and my hair feels limp even though the AC's set at sixty-eight. I notch it down and check my reflection in the rearview, but see Gracie.

"You're gonna remember to drink, right sweetie?"

She nods.

I read somewhere that millions of kids die each year from dehydration. That's worldwide, but still I worry. Soccer coaches are such fanatics. They almost never call games — even when I kindly suggest it's too hot. Gracie never complains.

"I love you, Little Fish," I say, and her reflection smiles. Chipmunk cheeks like her dad. Her tongue pushing into the hole where her canine tooth should be.

—

At the park, practice is just getting going. Two girls I recognize as Gracie's old teammates are running across the fields to the one nearest the lake: Field 6.

"Go ahead," I say. "I'll bring the gear." Soccer is good cross-training for swimming, but mostly it's a social thing for Gracie.

I sling my purse over my shoulder then loop on the folded camp chair in its canvas sheath, slide Gracie's duffle onto my other shoulder, grab the owl water bottle from the floor and shove it in the Thirty-One tote I'm gripping, as I kick the door shut and click the key fob with my free hand to lock up. Being a mom is like being a camel. We carry stuff. That's what we do.

Gracie did a report on camels once. We learned "camel" is derived from a Hebrew word, gamal, that among other things means "going without." Camels can go for weeks without drinking water because of adaptations — nostrils that trap water vapor, thick fur that insulates them and keeps them from sweating, and kidneys that reabsorb water more efficiently than other mammals. A camel survives the desert by holding on to every drop of water in her body.

I imagine myself a camel trekking across the desert as I trudge toward the field. I ignore the fact that the nylon band on the chair's holster is pressing my purse strap into my clavicle. A camel doesn't give in. A camel has a job to do. I tick through my mental checklist: Gracie's water bottle, her snack pack, my phone and e-reader, and the SPF 50 sun block. Can't have Gracie getting skin cancer and as an adult lamenting, "Mom! How could you?" Like Barry says, most emergencies are preventable. Plan. Prepare. Perform.

When finally I get to the sidelines, practice is in full swing. I set up my chair next to Susan Barrier. I recognize her from behind by her sheen of straight blond hair. Her daughter, Arianna, goes to school with Gracie. They're not best friends, but they're good friends. Gracie's been over to spend the night several times, and Ari's slept over at our house, too.

I situate myself with my book and straw hat, my prescription sunglasses and a snack-sized bag of almonds. "Hey Susan."

She wobbles in her seat when she sees me and nearly spills her Diet Sierra Mist. "Krystal! I'm … How are you?" She puts her hand on my arm. "It's so good to see you."

As if I haven't been hauling my girl to soccer practice every summer since forever. But I just mumble, "You, too," and am relieved when her clammy palm lifts from my bare arm. "Sure is a boiler for June," I say with as much perk as I can muster.

"Yeah." She smoothes her long, shiny hair behind one shoulder.

Kids scream and a mower's engine growls persistent and loud from a field I can't see. The smell of fresh-cut grass ripens the air. Because today is the first practice of the season, after warm up and a few drills, the girls start scrimmaging — just so the new coaches can see them play. We watch the girls kick the ball up and down the manicured green field. I gulp cool water from Gracie's owl bottle. I know she won't mind.

"Go, Ari!" yells Susan as her daughter shoots. She misses. "Next time, honey!" Susan sits back in her chair, eyes glued to the field, and takes a deep breath. "Krystal, I'm sorry I haven't called or stopped by. I just — you've been sorta holed up. If you ever wanna talk…"

Susan and I were on the Winterfest Committee together like two years ago and we see each other at soccer, but that's it.

"It's fine! We're fine." I swallow another slug of metallic-tasting water.

"But Gracie…"

"Did she leave something last time she was over?"

Susan's face turns completely white. I mean she's a ghost. And for a second, I wonder if she's choking on something. I've never given the Heimlich, but I think I'd know how. Like if Gracie was choking. But really, I don't want to expel a snack cracker from Susan's throat today.

"You okay?" I ask.

Susan shakes her head. She swallows. I watch her throat muscles contract and roll down her tan neck. I remember when Gracie learned that movement was called "peristalsis." She said, "It's when muscles in the throat move food down," and I said, "What about when you puke? Don't your muscles move food up?" She said, "Nope. You use your abdominal muscles when you barf. Peristalsis is just one way." Like the movement of time. A thing happens, and it's swallowed down.

I'm relieved that Susan's not choking, but she looks bothered. Sad, actually, as if she's about to cry, and just as I think this, little tears begin to pool in her lower lids. I'm terrified they'll slosh out any minute, and though that merciless hot sun is making me light-headed, I at least have the presence of mind to dig around in my purse for a tissue and hand it to Susan.

"Are you okay?" She's asking me.

"Totally!" I want to add, Better than you. I heard Susan and her husband were separated. Maybe they're getting divorced.

"How did Ari like fourth grade?" I ask, because all moms like to talk about their kids. If I can get her talking about Ari, maybe she'll feel better — at least long enough to get through practice and the BBQ without a total meltdown.

Susan perks up and begins describing Arianna's new pre-teen attitude, the girl's resistance to chores and homework, and how her hamster, Sandman, who is the color of yellow sand, sleeps all the time. "He's been a big disappointment," says Susan. "I wish I could lie around napping all day."

"I know what you mean."

Thankfully, practice runs only forty-five minutes on account of the BBQ.

—

The covered picnic area sits to the right of the fields and just up from the dock and swimming area. I'm relieved to see that one of the dads has brought a portable propane grill, so we don't have to use those gross on-site charcoal grills. Everyone knows meth addicts cook drugs on them in the darker hours.

Susan pulls a pack of Hebrew National beef franks out of her blue cooler.

"The good kind," I smile, dabbing the sweat off my forehead with a white paper napkin.

"Costco." She hands the hotdogs to a dad I don't recognize.

There was an accident at the end of last season. One of the kids was swimming with her dad in the lake. The girl got a side ache, I guess. She'd gone out too far and couldn't make it back. A freak accident. Anyway, several families left the team after that. This year, I see lots of new faces.

I walk out to the dock where the girls are splashing each other and jumping in. The air is cooler over the lake. Gracie has already changed into her tankini. The one with the blue top and the red-and-white striped bottoms. She looks like an American flag.

"We haven't forgotten her." I didn't notice Susan standing next to me.

"Who?"

"Number fourteen."

Fourteen was Gracie's number last year. They all got new jerseys this year. I'm not even sure what her number is now.

"That's why we stayed on the team," says Susan, who is smiling without showing her teeth.

"I used to worry about her," I say, watching Gracie. "But I don't anymore." My girl has such a beautiful stroke. The way her elbow crests the black water, and her pretty mouth takes in air, as if she's trying to gulp in the sun. My Little Fish was born to swim. I never worry about her in the water.

"You're a much stronger person than me."

From the picnic shelter Hot Dog Dad calls down to Susan for more of her "high-falutin franks."

Susan touches my arm. Again. With her sweaty hand. "I'm glad you came," she says for the second time and takes off toward Hot Dog Dad. The blunt ends of her hair swish back and forth as she strides away. She hurries up the sandy incline, eager to deliver those franks. The jewels on her jean pockets flash in the sun and her white tennis shoes gleam.

Maybe she really is getting divorced and she's got a thing for Hot Dog Dad. Even if it's true, I don't judge her. Marriages are frail, no matter how much you plan, prepare, and perform. Some men close off. Especially after a crisis. Maybe Ari's dad is like that.

The moment I think of Ari, her head emerges on the ladder near my foot. "Cold," she says, climbing up onto the dock, dripping and shivering, in her green, polka-dot one-piece. "Where's my mom?"

"Up helping with the food. She'll be right back." I don't know this for a fact, but as a rule, Mom's always come right back.

"I need my towel."

"Bet it's here somewhere." I scan the dock. Colorful beach towels are everywhere, some folded into squares, others hanging from the slats. "What color?"

"Red. It's a giant Coke can."

I find the towel and wrap it around Ari's shoulders. She looks into my face and I think she's going to thank me, but instead says, "I miss Grace."

"She's here," I say, kneeling.

"Yeah. In here," she points to her chest. "That's what mom says." She scrunches up her face. "But it's dumb. I think that's just something people say to make you feel better."

It's true. You hear the stupidest garbage when people are trying to make you feel better.

"I wrote her a secret note," whispers Ari. "When I first got Sandman. Me and Grace always wanted hamsters. I told her about how he's so fluffy and sleepy and cute."

"I write her notes, too," I say. "And I talk to her." Because I couldn't survive if I didn't. Because I lost myself that day.

Ari bobs her wet head up and down. Her face is nothing like Grace's, but there is something similar about her eyes, the shape, maybe or the seriousness in them. I miss Gracie so much. Her. Me. The old me. Barry. Life before. I wish everything would come back.

"I keep my notes," I say. "I hold on to every piece of her I can."

"I'm sorry," says Ari. "I threw my note away."

"That's all right," I say.

Susan huffs up next to us, red-faced and out of breath from running. "We gotta go, honey," she says to Ari. "Ballet at three."

Ari shakes her head and sighs. "I wish I'd kept that note."

I nod, but I'm looking past them both, to the lake where the water has turned Gracie's blond hair dark. The small roundness of her skull moves along the glassy lake, as if a pin is being pulled through the water by an invisible hand, and the surface ripples like peristalsis as she swims.

# CAELYN WILLIAMS

Caelyn Williams is a 24–year-old author and writer, someone who loves crafting the written word just for the sake of writing. Her first published work, *Eliza's Journal*, was released in the fall of 2012. When not writing, she spends her time enjoying the arts, researching, and just generally learning, with a side job of cat wrangling, i.e., volunteering care for feral felines.

Caelyn was born in 1990 in Portland, Oregon but has lived the majority of her life in Thurston County, Washington. Grown and raised in the Pacific Northwest, Caelyn has a great appreciation for the variety of wildlife, services, and cultures throughout our region. She doesn't even particularly mind the rain.

She currently resides in Lacey, Washington, amongst the lakes and trees.

# Mistakes Are Made

The moment Jane saw Soo Kim enter her office, carrying a large pet crate, she knew something was soon to go badly. Kim worked in Genetic Research and Testing Facilities, and Jane didn't trust even a lunch date with the man without worries of some sort of deadly disease spreading from him to her turkey sandwich.

When Jane took her job, she had expected a slightly more professional environment; what she got was a bunch of white-coated scientists on their fifth can of energy drink debating who could clone what more successfully. There were, of course, protocols they all had to subscribe to, regardless of the lab they were stationed in. These protocols went more ignored than a 'Employees must wash hands' sign in the bathroom of a fast food establishment.

"Jane. You look well!" Soo Kim greeted her with a smile that was full of teeth and lies.

"No," Jane said simply, turning back to the specimen sample that was waiting for her under the microscope. Kim's face fell, just for a moment, but he bounced back quickly enough.

"I haven't even said anything yet." Soo Kim responded, while hefting the pet carrier onto the countertop. "So, you heard about the Moa experiment?"

"I may have," Jane paused, casting a suspicious look at the pet carrier. "Are you telling me you successfully brought back a Moa? Is that what's in the carrier?"

"Well, see, that is the thing." Kim hummed; his smile was a bit tighter than it was before. "Carl, you know Carl? He may have mixed up samples, and we may have not noticed until they hatched."

Jane stared in horror, kicking one foot out to push her rolling chair away from the mystery creature that Soo Kim was intended to drop on her doorstep.

"Absolutely not. No."

"I haven't even asked yet, Jane. You're overreacting." Soo Kim sighed, leaning over to pull up the latch on the crate.

Jane pulled up her feet onto the chair, and grabbed a meter ruler for good measure. The ruler had a wickedly sharp metal edge, so it was as good protection as any.

"I don't want to see it, Soo!" She didn't get the option to not, as he swung the carrier door open and lifted the butt of the box so whatever beasty inside would slide out.

Out fell something white; that was Jane's first thought. Whatever it was stumbled awkwardly, obviously young because it wasn't supporting itself well. The head was much larger than the rest of its body, though it had an admirably long tail. It was roughly the size of a French bulldog, but looked like a python had tried to mate with a cockatoo. Jane noted leathery skin near legs and tail, combined with fluffy short down to be topped off with bunches of pin feathers around the back of the head. It didn't look quite like a reptile or any bird she had ever studied before. That was saying something, given Jane studied avian-borne diseases and parasites for a living.

"That isn't a Moa," Jane whispered in fear.

The thing in question tried to shimmy its way into a more upright position, flapping small arms and whacking that long thick tail like an angry cat. It finally made it up more firmly onto back legs, making a strange animalistic sound Jane had never heard before in the entirety of her life. It sounded rather like a macaw choking on a soda can.

"No, he's not a Moa." Kim agreed. "See, we were comparing DNA samples to older Avian species and some not so Avian. One got mislabeled, which ironically enough, we all had a good laugh about at first. I mean, we thought there would be absolutely no way anyone would be stupid enough to mistake that particular sample for Moa."

Soo Kim explained, absentmindedly reaching his hand out to scratch the little monster behind what appeared to be ear holes.

The muscles under its eye began to twitch, mouth falling open, and the whole thing tipped over onto its side. It kicked its back leg like a hound, and Kim seemed to not think much of the situation as he then went on to give belly rubs.

"What is it, Kim?" Jane snapped, knowing Soo's tendency to stroll around the park when it came to explaining anything remotely uncomfortable.

"Well, he's an albino, as you can tell. Very rare. Probably. This is a remarkable research opportunity, Jane." Kim was trying to bait her with pretty talk, and possible genes to play with.

"See, I wouldn't have even brought him, but his sisters tried to eat him. He's much smaller than they, and I'm already up to my armpits with the sisters. No one else lives here at the compound who knows as much about avian species as you do, Jane."

"Kim, it isn't a bloody bird! I know it's not a bird, because I know what a bird looks like, and that looks like, it looks like a stack of NDA's I'm going to have to sign, is what it looks like!" Jane's voice rose, which caused the thing to make a series of chirping noise in concern, trying to right itself again. Then something dawned on her.

"Did you say sisters? There are more of them?" Soo Kim ignored Jane's questions, carrying on.

"It'll just be a couple years, all food and supplies will be provided. Once he gets big enough, he'll be moved out of your house. Eventually, he'll get his own space to roam, free meals, and all it'll cost him is some blood, tissue, and saliva tests now and then. This is a huge opportunity, Jane. For us, for the world! Imagine how much information we'll get out of this guy, and his sisters. They could be the key to ending the Avian Plague Virus."

Kim cut a few corners here and there, not something you want in someone who can clone long dead creatures back from the beyond, but Kim wasn't a bad man and he wasn't nearly, well, he wasn't completely stupid. The Avian Plague Virus, or APV, for the last ten years had been wreaking havoc on bird populations worldwide. It wasn't a matter of birds simply getting sick; whole species were dying off at alarmingly fast rates. Common food fowl, like chicken and turkey, were also being hit hard. Prices soared as stock grew close to nothing, and it wasn't long until humans began to go hungry and starve. Meats, eggs, long gone. Once a cheap food source, now removed.

There was no antivirus, there was no cure yet invented, and the stakes were getting higher. There were a few isolated reports of avian to human virus transfers, and while it hadn't evolved to being able to transfer between human hosts, it was likely only a matter of time. Regardless, the food shortage itself was wiping out hundreds of thousands of people worldwide, just by itself.

"If I agree, will you at the very least tell me what it is?" Jane sighed, having gotten into her field of research for the sake of helping people. If there was any chance this might provide steps to a cure, Jane was willing to sacrifice her time and sanity to the cause.

"He's a dinosaur, Jane. That should be obvious." Kim's voice had a level of judgment to it, which Jane did not appreciate.

"I know it's a dinosaur, Kim. I picked up on that. Don't take that tone with me; of the two of us, who accidentally cloned a dinosaur? I'm certain it wasn't me."

"All right, point taken. Little guy is a T-Rex. Tyrannosaurus rex. Probably. He could be another tyrannosaurid, we aren't entirely certain, but T-Rex sounds better."

Kim spoke like he was telling her the breed of his dog was schnizterdoodle, instead of admitting their division has screwed up so badly they accidentally brought back to life one of the most feared apex predators in Earth history. Almost as if on cue, the albino hatchling let out a roar. Or, he tried to. It was more like a very small belch, resembling a gnome with a drinking problem.

"There are multiple film franchises telling me you are an idiot, and whoever in charge that is allowing this to happen is an even bigger idiot." Jane said flatly.

Soo Kim dropped a stack of paperwork on her desk, and handed her a pen.

"So, what does that make you then?" He asked, as she began signing non-disclosure agreements right and left.

"A damned fool."

"With a new pet," Soo Kim added with a grin.

Jane glanced down at the creature in question with a sneer curling up onto her face. The idea of babysitting an extinct species wasn't abnormal to her, no, not here; that didn't mean she had any experience with dinosaurs, let alone this particular type. Sure, she'd had great auk's and dodo's in her bathtub, even briefly spent a summer bottle feeding a young mastodon. The mastodon was not small, and it wasn't within her area of expertise either; but the very large difference is Jane did not have to worry about a baby mastodon chewing off her pinky toe in the middle of the night.

"I still don't understand why I have to keep it; can't someone down at the Carnivore lab deal with him?"

"Who do you think is taking care of the other sister?" Soo Kim responded. "You don't think I could take care of more than one of these guys, do you? I've got Sue. Sarah Longham has Kali. She apparently was looking forward to a break from the hyenas."

"Sue? Clever," Jane said with disdain, imagining Longham had been the one to name the other sister Kali.

Sarah Longham was brilliant, if not a bit odd, the Jane Goodall of animals that would rip your throat out. She was a brilliant woman in her field, and got along with most people she met, but no one wanted to invite her to dinner parties.

"I thought so — Jane, watch yourself." Soo Kim warned.

Jane glanced over at The Littlest Predator who had apparently taken a liking to the movement of her pen, sailing back and forth across paper. It was disconcerting to see the red eyes of rare albinism on an even odder creature; the red shone brightly as the pupils contracted down to pinpricks. Jane had seen the same mannerism on other bird species and reptiles, but very few of them would grow large enough to eat her in a single bite.

"He's perky. How long since he hatched?" Jane asked, not taking diligent eyes off of the tot-rex which was mimicking her hand motions with its head and dizzying itself.

"A week, give or take a few hours; I think I passed out for a while. Might have lost a bit of ear. Not from them, of course. Lemur, they're nasty little things." Kim pointed to an ear, which had a very pink strawberry print patch on it. Jane had noticed it when he came in the room, but chose not to comment on it; it wasn't her place to judge.

"How quickly do tyrannosaurs grow?" Jane asked.

"Don't worry; it'll be a good 2–5 years before you have to worry about not being able to handle him." Kim responded, looking like there was a longer story to be explained, one that Jane was not interested in hearing.

"Lovely. Now, if only I could trust a single word from you."

—

The compound in which they all worked was in an unlisted location in the Sakha Republic of Russia, stretching miles above and below ground. Their general isolation gave the company space to conduct experiments, while being far from the prying eyes of journalists. Workers, for the most part, lived in a small town made up of apartments and houses nearby, and would be transported into the facility. It was all very Area 51, and likely contained more secrets and less actual security.

People like Jane, a small handful of scientists, security and engineers, lived permanently on campus. Her spacious and sparse flat was within walking distance of the grand avian center, where she and her colleagues did their work. A small outdoor suspended walkway led from her flat to the upper levels of an extensive Aviary. Within, it felt like being in a rainforest, outside it felt the middle of nowhere Russia.

Soo Kim had provided Jane with a long list of dinosaur dos and do nots, which made her feel like she was babysitting a neighbor's dog instead of a 68 million year old creature.

— Dairy products: Not allowed.
— Vegetables and fruit: Unlikely he'd want any.
— Meat? Plenty of it.

Soo Kim, and the company, had delivered a locker full of vacuum-sealed meats of many different species, just to see which the young tyrannosaurus would prefer. Mammals wouldn't have been something any large dinosaur would have been eating, so no one was quite certain if mammalian meats would even be something they'd want to eat. Sharks preferred sea life to land animals; it was likely a Tyrannosaurus rex would prefer that which it would have been preying upon during the era it was alive. The problem being they didn't have access to that particular food source, the best-by date having past a few million years earlier.

That didn't mean there weren't some options open to them; fish and crocodilian meats were available and plausible choices. Ideally, poultry would have been a good replacement given the genetic similarities, but it just wasn't an option. Alligator and crocodile farms had been present before the APV struck, but the business boomed after. Seafood had already been becoming less of a common commodity due to overfishing; in hopes of being able to feed future populations, inland fish farms had become far more common.

Soo had informed Jane that after the babies had hatched, they had been fed on a diet of blended beef and alligator meat. It took no time at all before they were tearing apart the bottles and needing actual pieces of food. These meat sources had the benefit of being more easily accessible, and relatively inexpensive. It would become ever increasingly difficult to feed something that would grow to around 4–6 tons. Without a regular food source they risked injuring their research subject or accidentally creating a rather morbid game of hide and seek with Tyrannosaurus and intern.

——

A series of low clicks came from the pet carrier, as Jane placed it on the linoleum of her kitchen floor. Deep down she knew it wasn't honestly a threat, not now, not at this size; but deeper down, in some ancient mammalian part of her brain, Jane did not feel entirely comfortable with the creature. Still, logic won out over genetic memory, and Jane opened the crate.

The littlest tyrant came bobbling out quickly, making huffing sounds in its chest, before it seemed to notice it was no longer in the lab. He flattened himself down to the ground, unmoving, a familiar defense trait. Jane hadn't seen his sisters yet, but she imagined their coloring was likely more suited to camouflage, where as he was pure white and clashed rather terribly against the yellow floral pattern of the floor.

Jane shrugged it off and made towards the locker of dead meats, ignoring a pair of small red eyes that followed her movement. She decided on a chunk of alligator meat and a slice of raw tuna for his dinner. Her decision must have been a good one, when suddenly the albino tyrannosaur was off the ground and nipping at her pant leg. It was cute, in a strange way. Like a very strange and very mutated cat. Then he tried to scale her leg, and Jane was less amused.

"No. Down, you wee lizard." Jane ordered, and he didn't answer. He couldn't, given he had taken a sizable bite of pant fabric. He was desperately trying to get his legs up and climb, but the front limbs simply weren't long enough to grasp properly, so he just hung off the fabric suspended by powerful jaws.

"I need to give you a name, don't I?" Jane mumbled, shaking her leg just hard enough to dislodge the infant. She removed the wrappers from the chunks of meat, grimacing just briefly at the slippery texture, before holding it above the tyrannosaurus snout.

"Here you go, little mistake."

His pupils dilated, as he eagerly snapped at the food, downing the alligator quickly. He bit equally quickly at the tuna, but not all was rosy. He froze up, and then spit out the offending chunk of fish. Then, for good measure he stomped it further into mush on Jane's kitchen flooring.

"Okay, no tuna."

When he gurgled in response and belched loudly, Jane arrived at the rather fitting name of Bo: Body Odor.

—

Bo seemed intrigued by Jane's flat, but when the building was built, they hadn't counted on making it dinosaur friendly. He didn't particularly like the linoleum; claws clacked against it; the surface was cold, a far cry from the dirt and earth he'd have been adapted to. The carpeting was more agreeable, except when Bo went to roll on the softer material; his pinfeathers had the tendency to get snagged. Jane found herself more than once untangling a gurgling and unhappy baby tyrannosaur from the beige monstrosity.

Bo fell asleep at nearly 3 in the morning, conking out quickly after the excitement wore down. Jane wasn't so fortunate; she still had work to do. Bo wasn't a pet; he was an experiment, one a lot of research would be riding on. All of her interactions and observations would have to be cataloged, preferably before she passed out on the sofa and forgot them. So, Jane shuffled Bo back into his crate and got to work. She certainly wasn't about to let him roam freely.

Bo woke up before the birds did, eager and ready to be fed once again. Jane realized she must have nodded off at some point during the morning, awoken by the sound of rattling and gnashing of teeth. Moving from the kitchen table strewn with papers, Jane released Bo once more. He was out, running around, tripping over himself, and chirping at Jane expectantly.

"I guess you are a baby, after all." Jane mused.

Jane fed Bo another helping of alligator and this time accompanied it with a slice of bison. That, he ate much happier than the tuna. Deep down, Jane was mildly disconcerted watching, thinking that Bo was more than happy to eat mammalian animals. Bo, as he was now, was small and almost cute, but that would only last so long. How long would it be before he realized human beings were easy hunting?

Jane wasn't entirely sure what to do with Bo once work rolled around. She'd have to bring him with, but letting him openly run around the lab was a spell for disaster. It took a few minutes of brainstorming and calling ahead, but the decision was made to bring him to the enclosed aviary. It had other species of birds, a more hospitable environment, and more importantly, it had a small movable lab she could use. It wouldn't be the same extent of materials at her fingertips as Jane's usual lab, but this was the only way she could monitor the tyke while still allowing him enough freedom that she could work.

—

Jane hadn't been the only one who had thought of using the aviary, Soo Kim and weary assistant Erin Rodger beat Jane to the punch. Sarah Longham was nowhere to be seen; an emergency in the canine labs called to her attention first which left Soo and Erin in charge of both girls. They had the sisters on what appeared to be metal chained dog leashes attached to pet harnesses, not a terrible idea, though it looked rather ridiculous.

The sisters, Sue and Kali, were larger than Bo and seemed more self-assured in the new environment than Bo was. They nipped at each other, and at poor Erin Rodger's leg, before noticing Bo. They chirped, he grunted; they bristled and hissed, he hid behind Jane's leg. Siblings never changed.

Jane hadn't counted on how strange it would be to see the other Tyrannosaurus girls. They were a gingery orange to start with, odd in and of itself, made stranger by a dappling effect caused by nearly navy blue markings; white spots made their way down the top of the back and tail, while in addition to the blue, their faces and limbs had black bands like tiger stripes. They too had pinfeathers, but those colors had yet to be seen. Sue and Kali stood out, in other words, in a way that seemed strange for what was assumed to be a stealth predator. It was as if someone had thrown a macaw, tiger, crocodile, and peacock together into a blender just to see what would come out.

"Nice timing, Jane!" Soo Kim called, looking a bit more frazzled than Jane had last seen him. At the very least it was nice to see that they had been as much trouble for him to figure out as Bo had been for Jane. Without Sarah there to provide support, the genetic researcher was rather like a fish out of water. Kim didn't complain though; Jane had to hand it to him in that regard.

"We were just about to let them off leash, record and observe and then nap." Erin groused, shooting Kim a look down a hooked nose, though the look may have been more directed at the dinosaur triplets than her supervisor.

"Is that a good idea?" Jane asked, glancing down at Bo who had his large head smothered up against her leg in attempts to hide from mean sisters. "What about the other birds in the aviary, they could pose some risk couldn't they?"

"What? No, of course not! I mean, probably not. I don't think any of our flightless birds would attack them." Soo Kim chuckled, while Erin just sighed loudly and pointedly.

"I meant a danger to the birds, Kim" Jane corrected. She had already begun to notice a decrease in background noise, the birds in the area had already noticed the newcomers. The smarter ones had flown in to observe; crows and parrots were just barely visible from the trees nearby.

"Well," Kim began, shifting back onto the balls of his feet. "I suppose we'll just have to find out, won't we?"

—

Kim said after the fact, that everything had gone much better than expected. Soo Kim was, however, an idiot. The sisters, Sue and Kali, became little queens of the forests very quickly. Bo, on the other hand, tried to be at all times between Jane's feet. This wasn't so much due to fear of a new environment but because his interestingly colored siblings tended to grumble and snap at him if Bo grew too close. Jane couldn't be certain if sexual dimorphism was the cause for the sisters' disdain for their little brother, or if they didn't recognize him as one of their own due to his albinism. Jane did take pleasure in documenting the conundrum very thoroughly, however.

Watching Sue and Kali play, stalking through the woods, it was amazing to think that they hadn't the foggiest clue that the rest of their species was long gone. Of course, they weren't the only ones in this aviary with no other family on earth to speak of; many of the bird species here had been all but wiped out, and the humans themselves were edging towards the abyss. Yet, life carried on, the world would keep spinning, and life would hopefully continue on to create more than it destroyed.

"Needle time!" Soo Kim announced happily, as his assistant wheeled in a medical cart.

As the hours passed by, Sue and Kali had apparently gotten over much of their disdain for their brother and began allowing Bo into some of their reindeer games. The three tyrant tykes stayed close to their human adopted parents, but played games much like any young animal would. They wrestled, leapt over logs and rocks, ran around tree trunks, and waited to pounce from long grasses and bushes. Eventually, the excitement began to wear off, and, much like kittens and puppies, the three baby dinosaurs found themselves deeply asleep in a large pile. It was cute, because they had no idea they were about to be jabbed repeatedly with medical equipment.

Erin picked up Sue first, the smaller of the sisters, and far less trouble than Kali. The lot of them were exhausted enough from playing, so much so that Sue didn't react with more than a low unending grumble over being picked up, much like an ornery pug. Sue was curled up on her back, her large head flopped back in Erin's arms; Erin was careful not to bend back any delicate pinfeathers; she had learned her lesson the hard way already. Sue didn't react to the pain of the needles, though it made sense as to why; with siblings who already had teeth bigger than human canine teeth, a Tyrannosaurus rex would have to be fairly used to rough treatment.

Or so they thought until handling Kali. Kali took far more offense over the process, having woken up to watch her sister manhandled. She spent the entire time silent, simply watching with clever eyes, until Kali's own turn came. Jane had to help Soo Kim fit Kali with a small muzzle when it came time for her blood samples. Kali snarled, thrashed, and her pinfeathers shook and stood up in what would likely have been a dramatic display once she was fully grown.

Bo, however, didn't even notice. He stayed asleep, amongst the prodding and needles and weighing. He didn't even grumble when it came time for a cheek swab. In the back of her mind, Jane was glad it seemed like she had ended up in charge of the calmest of the three. Then, the forefront of her mind reminded Jane that she shouldn't have had to deal with any of them, if only Kim and his colleagues had had a brain between them.

"That should do it," Kim mumbled, agitating the last sample. "Erin, can you get these off to Emerson and Martinez?"

"I relish every opportunity I am given not to be here." Erin drawled, grabbing the handle of the cart. Erin was generally rather morose, but Jane couldn't blame her for it. The genetics lab had a tendency to wear everyone out.

"In a few days, we should have preliminary results back." Kim told Jane, after Erin left with the samples. The two left had no time to rest, not when work was still to be done, not when babysitting Cretaceous-era beasts.

"Results regarding their immunity to the Avian Virus, I'm guessing?" Jane didn't bother to look up from her papers.

"Right. Call me optimistic, but I'm hoping for the best. If the results are promising, we can start doing actual tests." Kim sighed, stretching his legs and arms out in a big show. He looked more tired than ever but very nearly happy about it.

"I'm not sure how you managed that optimism, Soo, but I admire the spirit," Jane admitted, thinking of grabbing a pot of coffee. They both needed it.

"You don't think they'll be of any help?" Kim asked, eyebrows tipping up. Jane shrugged a shoulder at the question.

"I'm sure they'll be of some scientific relevance. Just the fact you've managed to bring back something this old is amazing in and of itself. But I can't say I have much faith in regards to them solving the APV. They're too old, Soo. Too far back. I doubt it would even infect them." Jane stated plainly, not one to hide her thoughts.

"I disagree." Kim said airily, waving her comments off. "You'll see. It's fate."

"Your concept of fate concerns me."

—

It was the weekend, and while weekends didn't mean much around these parts, Jane was enjoying an early evening off from work. Falling into an easy pattern, Jane was far more comfortable around her dinosaur ward, as seen by the fact that while she was in bed reading, Bo was curled up next to her, absentmindedly gnawing on a uncooked bone. Bo wasn't allowed to sleep on the bed yet, he wasn't potty trained, if potty training was even possible, but refusing to let him up onto the bed resulted in hour-long whining and clawing of the sheets.

He couldn't have imprinted the same way many bird species did, but Bo was undeniably attached to Jane in a way he wasn't to his siblings. Maybe it came from the fact she fed him, and he was just a baby, but Jane suspected Tyrannosaurus rex was in fact a pack animal. Bo was social, remarkably so, though Jane was not. This was why she spent her time off in her room, rather than in town or at the lab.

The call came at half past 9. Jane had her suspicions who would be calling, which is why she let it ring a few times before answering. That, and Bo very much did not care for her ring tone and immediately went into a crouched defensive stance with all of his little pins and downy feathers puffed out like a fat little bird.

"I told you so!" These were the first words out of the speaker, when Jane finally answered the phone. She hung up immediately. It rang again.

"Has anyone ever told you that your people skills leave something to be desired?" Soo Kim's voice came through clearly, so Jane hung up again. This time, when it rang, she answered and spoke first.

"Your people skills leave something to be desired, Soo."

"Yes, well, there is a reason I'm in genetics and not the social sciences. Anyway, I have more to say. I told you so. There, I said it." Jane could very nearly see his grin, with the image his voice painted.

"There is a reason you're not in the humanities either, I'd wager. Care to explain further?" Jane ignored the vast urge to sigh, while shifting the phone to her other ear so that she could more easily put her book down. Bo was watching with interested eyes, tilting his head when

65

he heard Soo Kim's voice, not knowing where the other person was speaking from.

"Tests are back, and looking very promising. They're not immune to the APV samples, but the virus doesn't have anywhere near the same effect it does on our avian species." Kim sounded excited, just on the phone, like a little boy in a plagued candy shop.

"Really? That is interesting. The virus really shouldn't be able to infect them. Humans have been the only other species infected." Jane paused in thought, wondering what the possible ramifications would be. Not just in terms of the virus, but if Bo and his siblings were immune, it would very likely mean the higher ups would want to begin cloning more dinosaur species to test. Somehow, that seemed like a bad idea.

"Theropoda, Jane. Birds evolved from them, Tyrannosaurus rex is one. It makes perfect sense, do you see that now? This is the beginning of a cure!" As Soo spoke, Jane could just barely hear the sounds of twin chirps in the background, indicating that Soo had both Sue and Kali with him again.

"Is Longham with you? What does she think of all this? I'm sure you're as aware as I am that this likely means more tests and more dinosaurs. I don't want to babysit more dinosaurs, Kim."

"She's here. Sarah is all for it! She'd very much like a Gorgonopsid, but I had to remind her we're focusing on Theropods." Kim paused, and Jane could hear the sound of someone muttering on the other line, just briefly. "Ah, but she said she'd settle for a Carcharodontosaurus."

"They're bigger than Tyrannosaurus rex! No! Go smaller than car-sized, Kim." Jane huffed, sitting up straighter. It'd be just like the genetics lab to use this as an excuse to start some sort of theme park attraction. That could never, ever, be a good idea.

"Car-sized, you say." Kim's voice was teasing, but it did nothing to help Jane's nerves. "Relax Jane; I can hear you grinding your teeth from here. We're going to focus on continuing tests with these three, then if it continues to go well, go for more recent species of Theropod. Smaller, so we can formally monitor them. No one wants to unleash packs of Utah raptors onto the populace, except maybe Carl."

Jane looked down at Bo, who was still focused on the noises coming from the phone, with a nearly glassy eyed expression.

"Do continued tests include purposely infecting Bo, Kali, and Sue?" Jane asked, not liking the thought of it. She couldn't deny that a world without three tyrannosaurs would likely be a better one, but still, infecting them while they were still babies didn't sit right either.

"Eventually, yes. Not right away. Not for another half year, to a full year. Depending on how quickly they grow. Sue would be first anyway. Kali is larger and healthier looking, but she scares me a little. Bo is a genetic oddball and the only male. So, Sue is first." Kim had to be confident if he was willing to test Sue, but Jane wasn't certain if he was confident in the results, or just ahead of himself and overly optimistic.

"She could die, Soo." Jane stated simply, he should know that much. It would have been better if the triplets couldn't be infected by the APV. Blood tests were one thing; actually infecting the host was another. There would always be risks involved.

"I know, Jane. I know."

—

By the time a year had passed by, Bo's head reached Jane's mid-thigh in height. Bo also happened to be still the smallest of the siblings.

Kali took an impressive first place in both height and weight, nearly a head taller than Bo, and a good 50 pounds heavier. Her stature was made more impressive by the fact that pinfeathers were long gone, replaced by real plumage. Kali had a mane of black feather, all tipped in peacock blue and green tones. It was a royal headdress fit for a ruler, which Kali very much was. She reigned over the aviary, she extended terror across the mammalian labs, but thankfully even Kali answered to someone: Sarah Longham. Kali dared not question her adopted mother. No one knew if this was for the best, as Sarah was far from tamed herself. Kali actually seemed to have picked up predator traits from the other animals Sarah looked over, hunting abilities neither Sue nor Bo had. Though Kali did try her best to teach her siblings, it was all for naught. She was very disappointed in her brother and sister.

Sue had gone through her own process; at half a year old Soo Kim had begun the real experiments. Sue was infected by the Avian Plague Virus, and then quarantined until all signs of the virus were gone. It hadn't gone smoothly at first; Sue had become rather listless the first week. She had a fever, and wasn't particularly interested in eating. For some time, Bo actually surpassed his sister in weight. But her immune system finally defeated the virus inside her, and after 3 very stressful months, Sue was given a clean bill of health. Soo Kim has been ecstatic, as was Sue, because she quickly retook her second place title back from Bo. While not as large as Kali, and far more docile, Sue was still definitely a force to be reckoned with. Sue was rather like a Great Dane, Jane thought. Sue was more than happy to try and curl up on someone's lap, usually Soo Kim's, while ignoring the fact she was far too large to do so. Kim never seemed to mind, he'd likely still let her even once she hit 7 tons.

Sue was not the end of experiments; she was just the beginning. With her, came the real possibility of a future vaccine. Immunity, a new vaccination, was on the horizon. With this in mind, the genetics lab went a bit mad with power. They were given the go ahead with further experiments in the hopes of further progression of the creation of a cure. That and the people who owned their secretive compound in the middle of Russia didn't care very much about following protocol. All business was rather chaotic neutral around these parts.

So, the inevitable happened. Dinosaurs happened. So, very, very many dinosaurs; Epidendrosaurus, Archaeopteryx, Oviraptor, Avimimus, Enantiornithes; along with small fleets of other small Theropoda and distantly related avian cousins. A new aviary had to be built, to hold primarily nothing actually avian. Trials began on the smaller dinosaurs, and the majority were immune, except for the Enantiornithes which were far more closely related to current bird species. The individuals who didn't die from the Avian Plague Virus, along with Sue's samples, began the next far more dangerous phase of creating a vaccine to use on modern bird populations.

They hadn't actually planned on purposely infecting Kali or Bo right away, but circumstances changed very quickly once Kali ate an infected smaller Theropod, and shared her meal between siblings. Neither experienced the same sort of flu like symptoms as Sue had, but for the short amount of time both were sick neither Jane nor Sarah Longham got much rest. Not due to worry, no, due to Bo and Kali both demanding constant attention and affection from their adopted human mothers. It was three long days and nights of special feedings, the softest blankets known to man, and dealing with sick dinosaur odor. Not a pleasant experience for anyone involved; even Jane's coworkers avoided her for a time, just due to the smell she carried around with her.

The dinosaurs quickly became an attraction just among the employees and their families, but the reasoning for creating the new enclosures fell on Tyrannosauruses' backs. They were ultimately wild animals, of a strange sort, and keeping them inside apartments and labs wouldn't be a good idea even if they weren't going to grow to be bus-sized. Eventually even the new enclosure wouldn't be large enough, but they wouldn't burn that bridge for some time.

For the time being, Jane would just try to enjoy the peace and quiet. With a vaccine in the making, individuals within the compound began to spread rumors, and those rumors escaped out into the general public until it seemed as though everyone on the planet had heard. Jane knew better than most now how close they were getting to creating an actual cure that could be dispensed out into the world. There were going to be problems, road bumps, no doubt about it, but for the first time in years, Jane was content. While species were still dying, and humans were still feeling the brunt of that fact, hope was just on the horizon. They might not be able to save everyone, surely not, but they could finally stop the Avian Plague Virus. And those who died, could now be brought back. A testament to this fact was the ever present ghost near Jane, Bo. His family had been reborn onto this planet after 65 million years, and he and his sisters were thriving.

"Bo, no." Jane huffed, grabbing the spray bottle off her side table to spritz the tyrannosaur in the face. Hope was indeed within sight and currently chewing on yet another pair of her nice shoes.

———

Five years brought a vaccine, one that worked, one that could be used upon any bird populations still in existence. However, administering the vaccine was difficult; injections were not the ideal form of distribution for flocks of anything, let alone things that could fly away when startled. Jane's lab and colleagues were working on creating a more easily consumed form, via some sort of liquid or feed, that would ease the process and make it easier to administer to wild pockets of surviving species.

Five years brought big changes for the three tyrannosaurus tykes, too, primarily the fact that they were now quite big themselves. Longer than an adult human, with a height that reached chest for Bo, and shoulders for Kali; they hadn't been fit for apartment life for years. Sue, however, still insisted she fit on Soo Kim's lap. He still allowed her to make such attempts.

None of the three acted quite like dogs or quite like cats or like birds or reptiles. They were their own strange category, and their aptitude for learning meant each behaved slightly differently even when faced with the same situation. Kali, due to Sarah's influence, enjoyed solitary hunting like the big felines she had encountered. However, when met with Bo and Sue, they all instantly switched back into pack hunter mode. Bo was more than happy to scavenge, usually having to wait his turn after his sisters anyway. Bo was the most docile as well, getting along with most. Sue loved Soo and not many other people which would become increasingly dangerous as she got bigger. Worrisome, yes, but thoroughly entertaining to document. Jane, though, was not known for her sense of fun.

None of the five-year-olds enjoyed their move from homes to an enclosure that did not have space heaters nor cuddle blankets. They adapted quickly as it was more like their natural habitat anyway, creating many little pockets where all three could sleep in a pile and share heat like normal nest-mates would. It helped that carnivore enthusiast Sarah Longham was more than likely to be found also sleeping somewhere in the enclosure, preferring the ground and moss to apartment life anyhow.

Deep down, Jane rather missed having Bo in her apartment, after having spent the better part of 5 years raising him there. There had been difficult times, destruction of valuables and bathtubs, but Jane saw Bo nearly as she would a child. He was her responsibility; Bo depended on her to learn about the wide world around them and how to interact with it. Jane was responsible for making sure Bo stayed safe and happy. Those responsibilities hadn't vanished, and Jane still spent the majority of her days around Bo and the others, but it just wasn't the same.

Jane was not a social person, and Bo was not the type of company you could carry on conversations with, but she still found herself getting lonely. More and more often Jane reached out, inviting colleagues over for tea or coffee, going out on lunch dates. Still, she found herself lonesome. That was, until Soo Kim delivered a new proposition.

—

By Bo's 10ᵗʰ birthday, he had grown to be the height of Jane. That didn't mean the albino saw her as anything other than his mother. He could easily kill her if he wished to, but Jane had never suffered more than a few stitches from an overly excited young dinosaur. Bo wasn't one to attack anyone at all, while he still roughhoused with his larger siblings and some of the larger animals in the facility, Bo wasn't about to actually injure any humans on purpose. Jane was thankful for this fact and for Bo's intelligence, because there was a new addition to the facility that was far more delicate than anything they had ever dealt with before. Jane wasn't certain how Bo would understand, or know how to behave around something his species would have never interacted with during the Cretaceous.

This strange little creature that thoroughly befuddled Bo, was none other than a human child. This is what resulted from Soo Kim's proposition, or rather, proposal. It had taken some convincing to move in with Soo, but Jane had been fed up with her now-empty apartment. Maybe it hadn't been the best thought-out life changing decision, but after raising an infant Tyrannosaurus rex, how difficult could living with Soo Kim be? Life wasn't so simple that such a change would be easy, but it was good the way it was. After living together for a few years, the news came that Jane was pregnant. Soo was thrilled; Jane was queasy for so very many reasons, but once their daughter was born, Jane couldn't imagine why she ever had any doubts in the first place. Well, strike that, Soo wanting to name their daughter Sue Junior was one reason for a handful of doubts.

Their daughter, Nadia, was born into a world where birds still flew in the sky. She would be part of a generation of humans who hadn't experienced the terror and worry of the Avian Plague Virus. Nadia would be one to help the world rebuild, after having lost much of many species' populations. She was also born to a generation to which dinosaurs once again walked the earth, for better or worse with repercussions likely not to be seen for years. The dinosaur species, as of now, were still primarily contained to the area near the compound or within. No large species were bred, no large carnivores, with the exception of Kali, Sue, and Bo. Go big or go home, Soo would say. But Soo was an idiot, as Jane would say.

It was interesting, watching Bo trying to interact with a toddler. He was a gigantic carnivorous-looking cockatoo-type creature; Nadia had pigtails and little bows. Nadia was quite fond of Bo's tail feathers, and Bo was not fond of his tail feathers getting yanked on, but Bo knew better than to injure Nadia. Nadia, Jane thought, in Bo's mind was likely seen as part of the pack. To Bo, she was a small little strange tyrannosaur that needed to be protected, even if she was odd looking and did not know how to hunt. Nadia was like a playful hatchling that tried to climb onto his back, which Bo also did not care for. Sue, however, quite liked Nadia. All three of the tyrannosaur triplets had been fixed early; they would never breed, but Sue became very much a big sister to Nadia. Jane was worried that Nadia might actually begin to see Sue and Bo as much her family as she saw Jane and Soo. Her teething period had been remarkably difficult for everyone.

Overall, things went well, remarkably so in fact. The dinosaurs all had their own extensive addition to the compound, and Bo and his sisters had acres of land to live on. Kali wasn't as sociable, but everyone now working in the Paleontology labs remained limbed and biteless. The three still had a ways to go in terms of growing; they weren't even half their adult size yet, but fear had disappeared. Kali, Sue, and Bo were now known and seen worldwide as what saved humanity, and maybe even the natural balance of the rest of the planet. They were three gigantic mistakes with wonderful ramifications.

—

Years later, Jane found herself sipping coffee on the veranda of their home just watching the flocks of birds flying overhead. Nadia was off somewhere, likely in the woods with her much larger adopted siblings. Soo was at daycare with Suzy, their second child who was as close to allowing the name Sue Junior as Jane would permit; which meant Jane finally had some peace and quiet in an otherwise busy home in the Sakha republic.

Then, a large white head rose from a thicket of trees off in the distance.

"Bo," Jane beckoned, waving a hand.

Bo roared in response. It still sounded rather like a large belch, but it wasn't Jane's place to judge.

# BETH ANDERSON

Beth Anderson is an author
and artist living in Olympia,
Washington with her husband
and two youngest children.
She has been published in
the *Saturday Evening Post*
and was acknowledged in the
top twenty-five New Writer's
Contest by *Glimmer Train*. She is
currently working on a Young
Adult novel set in Iceland.

# Hush, Now

My grandfather, a fiercely private man born in the nineteenth century, could never have imagined his personal life would be posted and available to any yahoo out there for thirty-two dollars a month. I guess at this point he has moved on.

During an innocent search on one of those genealogy websites, an unbeknownst relative appeared. I only wanted to see my ancestry line like the celebrities on that TV show. Really, I hoped to find a connection to the Salem Witch Trials. No witches so far, but I haven't finished looking; I know they are out there somewhere. The trouble was, I found an unknown uncle. On my mother's side. Again. Seems her father had another family she had found out about after his death. As an only child she was thrilled to find her half-sisters still living on the East Coast, odd elderly spinsters, but sisters nonetheless.

The website glaringly exposed my grandfather's previous wife and listed my mother's half-sibs with their birthdates neatly typed on the form. No big surprises. I recall seeing the old copy of our family tree with a thick, black band of ink drawn over the previous wife. Ah, those were the days, when an inch or two of white-out could solve a multitude of problems.

My only memory of my grandpa Walter is of sitting together on a big, covered porch in Dayton, Ohio. I was about six and putting stamps into a child's stamp book and he was breathing. He gazed down at the small, green valley in front of us. White horses grazed peacefully. I don't remember talking to him due to the lung machine the size of a refrigerator to which he was attached. Occasionally, he would take the mask off and enjoy a pipeful of sweet cherry tobacco that I can still smell sometimes. At the age of six, I saw nothing wrong with this and neither did he.

I was conjuring up that rich, tobacco smell when a tantalizing little icon swirled up on the screen asking me if I wanted to see something else. Well, do ya? It seemed a little condescending. Only a middle-aged woman in her newly empty nest would go this far anyhow. The last of my three kids recently left for college in a blur of loud music and hair straighteners. I really had to find something better to do than plot our family tree. It was that TV show that started the whole thing.

Without hesitation, I clicked onto the mysterious icon and waited patiently while the screen produced a copy of an old, hand-written record of people and their households in a 1919 census. In tidy, cursive handwriting that you don't see anymore, my grandfather's name was listed, then a wife, Sophia. Sophia. What an exotic name, after weeks of looking at Ebenezers and, I kid you not, Ichabods. "Swine flu" was scrawled under the "died" section for poor Sophia. My heart sank. I had just met her. The date was a few years before his marriage to a second wife, my grandmother coming in a distant third.

I was so excited to discover this wonderful tidbit about this man hooked up to the fridge/breathing machine, I almost missed the sweetest thing of all. A baby. Baby Walter. Another half-sib for my mother. I never thought of these people as related to me. My first thought was to call her. Then it occurred to me, maybe all these "surprises" were becoming difficult for Mom. My second thought was, he could still be alive.

Feeling no less than Nancy Drew herself, I entered the baby's name in a search. A matching result came up so quickly there wasn't even time to bite my fingernails. There it was, Walter Z. Burroughs, born 1918, Salem, Mass. I broke the news to my Yorkshire Terrier who showed overwhelming enthusiasm, wagging and panting at the discovery. Now what?

I went to the online white pages and there he was again, ninety-three years old, from Massachusetts, living in Tacoma, WA. Tacoma! Really! Not thirty minutes away from my home? What a strange coincidence. With a shaky hand, I wrote down the address and phone number. The site indicated that it was a nursing home in an area I was not familiar with.

When my husband came home that evening I bombarded him with my news. "I have an uncle." Since both of my parents were supposedly only children, my family tree is an extremely tall, thin one, a towering pine perhaps. My husband's is more like family groundcover so I don't think he could possibly feel my excitement at this discovery.

"Call him," he said casually as he stabbed a scalloped potato. I don't know if he even likes scalloped potatoes. It was the kids' favorite.

"Is it a good idea to call a ninety-three year old man and rock his world at this point?" I pondered. I pictured my frail grandfather withering away at the end of an oxygen tube like the last tomato on an October vine.

"I say call him. He's your uncle, after all. Good dinner, by the way." He wiped his mouth, gave me a quick smile and headed for the garage to work on his never-ending wood project. Soon, the sander growled in the distance while I cleared our few dishes off the table.

I thought about calling my daughter, Chloe, at college to see what she recommended, but I knew her answer would be, "Go, go meet this man now!" Which was not a bad idea. He may not be around much longer. I thought I would be adventurous and call her after I did this brave and outgoing thing.

The next morning was a Tuesday, as good as any. I kissed my husband good-bye and rinsed out the coffee press. Walter's phone number sat on the counter. I wiped down the stovetop then started pulling things out of the refrigerator to be tossed. Enough, I thought, holding a half-empty jar of sauerkraut. "I'm being a wimp," I told the dog. He heard, "Do you want a cookie?" and started bouncing maniacally up the cabinets towards his treat bag. It was enough encouragement for me.

I picked up the phone, gave the dog a cookie and quickly dialed the number. It rang once and I hoped I would get an answering machine to at least try out my voice.

"Sunset Nursing Home. May I help you?" asked a deep, female voice rough with the sound of years of hard work and maybe a few cigarettes.

"Yes, I am trying to reach Walter Burroughs." I curled my hair with my fingers, a nervous habit I haven't done in twenty years.

"Certainly." The voice sounded curious. "May I tell him who's calling?"

"Ok. My name is Jan Wilmitsky, but he won't know me."

"Just one minute, dear."

I waited while big band music played in my ear. I pictured Walter, in a black suit, with a silver cane, seated in an elegant concert hall enjoying the music while an usher taps his shoulder to inform him of my interrupting call. Instead, another female voice, this one softer, came over the line. "This is Dolly."

My heart pounded in my chest. "Oh hello. This is Jan Wilmitsky. I'm trying to reach Walter Burroughs." He must have refused to leave the concert hall.

"I'm Mr. Burroughs' nurse. He's sleeping now. Can I take a message?"

I was afraid of sounding like a crazy person. These women seemed a little protective of my precious uncle.

"Oh, yes, sure. Like I said, my name is Jan Wilmitsky."

"Got it."

"And I believe I may be Mr. Burroughs' niece."

"Really?" The nurse sounded optimistic but quite cautious.

"It shows in the records I have recently uncovered that he is my uncle from his father's side. I would like to come and talk to him if that's possible." I hated how my voice rose up at the end like a question. He was possibly family after all. I lowered my voice, kind of like Oprah's, and gave her my phone number.

"I'll give him the message," Dolly said in a professional manner.

By the following afternoon I had received a phone call back from Dolly and had a meeting arranged for four o'clock the next day. Old people have to move fast. No time to waste. Four o'clock, tea time. Yes, he was definitely one of us.

My wardrobe had taken a slow, downward spiral in the last ten years. Finding something suitable proved quite difficult. The dark green skirt, a little tight since the last time I wore it, with a loose, brown sweater went best with my unruly red hair and freckles. Looking in the mirror I remembered to put on sunscreen. Even in the weak, fall sun I could get a sunburn just waiting in line for a movie ticket.

I used my GPS to navigate my way through Tacoma. Funny, I've lived my whole life on the Puget Sound yet never had been on these busy streets with so much chain-link fencing and young people walking about in the middle of a weekday.

The Sunset Nursing Home sign was faded and a bit crooked but I was glad to have found it. A vicious-sounding dog gurgled at me from behind a screen door across the street. I double locked my car and hurried to the entrance. My feet weren't accustomed to the 'dressy' shoes I wore. I concentrated on walking properly along the cracked cement.

There is a smell to nursing homes that can't seem to be avoided. The musty odor of bedridden people hit me as I opened the door, an 'end of life' smell. We will all get there someday, I suppose. I hope I don't recognize it when it surrounds me.

"Afternoon," said the gruff voice. It came from a gray-haired black woman who, if she wasn't sitting at the front desk with a headset on, could have been one of the patients. She looked at me curiously. Her nametag read, "Mrs. Wilson."

I bustled up to her desk and put my clinking set of keys in my little 'dress' purse. Two well-worn chairs sat by the wall with a small, round table between them. A grayish doily lay centered on the table. It wasn't really a waiting room, more like a resting spot.

"I'm here to see Mr. Walter Burroughs at four o'clock," I said, cheerfully.

"You are his niece?" Mrs. Wilson's eyebrows shot up and wrinkled her forehead considerably. She lifted her bifocals off her heavy bosom and put them on to get a better look at me. I supposed they had to be careful of people claiming to be relatives trying to get into a last minute will.

I smiled openly and let her inspect me from behind the bifocals. "Yes. I am Jan Wilmitsky."

Mrs. Wilson grinned. "He will be so happy you are here. You know, he has never had any relatives. An orphan in this world, poor soul. Nicest man you will ever meet, though. He's very special to us. He has talked about nothing else since you called." She nodded toward the tired chairs. "Please have a seat."

Relieved to hear that he was taking this news so positively, a weight lifted off my shoulders. He wanted to meet me.

Mrs. Wilson punched a button on her phone. "Dolly, come up here quick. Mr. Burroughs' niece is here."

Several women in somewhat matching white uniforms came from the hallway, whispering to each other and sneaking peeks at me. I was touched by the interest the others were taking.

A beautiful Hispanic woman, about my age, marched efficiently toward me in her big white nurse shoes. I stood and adjusted my snug skirt, my hands shaking slightly.

"Hi there. I'm Dolly." She smiled. "Walter is right back here. Follow me."

We passed two other rooms in the hall. In one, a miniscule person, looked like a woman, with permed, white hair stacked up on her pillow and enormous, plastic-framed glasses covering most of her face, watched a talk show on a television perched in the upper corner of the room like in a hospital. The other room contained a bed with a person sleeping under a blue blanket with an IV tube emerging and snaking up a stand. I wondered if Walter would be hooked up to tubes.

"Mr. Burroughs?" Dolly poked her head in the next door. "Your niece is here."

"Please send her in this instant," boomed a voice so deep I could feel it through my dress shoes.

Dolly stepped aside and I approached the bed, trembling slightly. A very old, very tall, very black man sat upright in his crisp, white bed sheets. He held out a huge, ash-colored hand toward me. His milky white eyes stared dreamily in my direction.

I stopped in my tracks. Could we be distantly related? Maybe if his mother was black and Grandpa was… no, his mother would have had to have been purple and Grandpa would have had to be an albino to cause such a difference between us. I was about to say, "I'm afraid there's been a mistake," when Dolly took my hand and reached it to his, hanging in space. "Please," she said softly.

"There you are, Child." His face broke into a show-stopping smile. His sightless eyes leaked tears in the outer corners.

He covered my hand in his. His skin was soft and warm. "However did you find me?" His big voice wavered. "I looked for family my whole life and found nothing but disappointments. And here I am, at the end of my days, and who would have thought, a niece."

Strangely enough, tears sprang from my eyes as well. I spilled over with all my information. It was so wonderful to share it with someone who actually listened. I told him how I traced "our" family tree from old records on the internet. All the way from Massachusetts and his mother's tragic death of the swine flu and how his father, my grandfather, apparently couldn't raise a newborn on his own. How my mother and father moved to Seattle to start a family.

He nodded and listened and shook his head and smiled. "My adoptive parents told me about my mother dyin' so young. I didn't realize it was the swine flu. Dad was always a mystery, though. So my father went on to have more children. I suppose that's only natural. I'm happy for him." He took a deep breath. "I'll be seein' him soon enough and we can catch up then. He won't believe we met each other. This life is strange, isn't it?"

"Yes. Lord it is," I agreed. I can't believe I just tried to sound black. Did I really do that? "How did you end up over here in Tacoma?"

"Oh, I had a good childhood, raised by a couple in Salem. I didn't even know I was adopted until I was about grown. Didn't matter. Lovely people, my parents. I got a bit of an education, then I joined the service and traveled the world." His eyes sparkled in the sunlight streaking through the blinds. "When I retired, I traveled the world again, on my own terms. I have had a wonderful life."

We talked about things we enjoy doing. Reading and history were our biggest hobbies. He had an old tape recorder on a cart with a stack of books-on-tape beside it. He was in the middle of a novel I had just finished the week before.

"Aren't genetics something? I was a bit of an artist before I lost my sight," he said proudly. "Do we have any more in the family?"

I excitedly pulled out pictures of my three children and fanned them in front of him. I told him about the drawing classes I take and my daughter who is minoring in art. He ran his long fingers over their faces. "I'm sure they are beautiful," he said.

"They are," I said. "I will bring them in to meet you over Christmas break. They're all in college now."

"Smart kids. Three of them, too. What a blessing. I never slowed down long enough to have my own. Had a wife for thirty years, though. Brought her here from Thailand. She passed away in '98." He fumbled beside his bed and picked up a frame with a picture of a Thai woman with a big grin on her face as if he had just said something a little racy to her. He handed it to me. "Nim. You would have loved her," he said with a little laugh because I swear he remembered what he told her in that picture. "She would have loved you."

I ran my fingers over her face, like he did, as I studied her. "She's gorgeous, Walter."

"Oh, she was so much more than that," he sighed.

Looking at her picture and his face full of contentment I knew this couple had soaked up every bit of life that came their way.

I hardly noticed the soft footsteps of the aides checking in on us as we talked away into the evening. Finally, Dolly came into the room. "I hate to interrupt you, but you will need to eat something before you go to sleep, Walter." She looked at me with such warmth I thought she was going to hug me.

"Was he all you had hoped for?" my husband asked as we got ready for bed.

"And more," I said. "I'm going back on Friday."

"Still more to talk about, eh?"

"There is a lifetime of stuff to talk about," I said.

I brought my sketchbook with me on Friday and spent the afternoon drawing my uncle's animated expressions as he told me about Venice and Moscow. He told me how Nim, a confident woman who spoke a little English, saved him from the mistake of wearing his shoes inside a Thai Buddhist temple and then, after much persistence on his part, accepted his invitation to dinner. From then on, she joined him on the rest of his travels. He described the strange fruit in Bali and the nutty, sharp cheeses in Italy. We laughed so hard about our mutual dislike for Indian food that the aides came rushing in. He insisted it was okay for me to stay while he ate his mushy dinner. I could see his face become droopier and his movements a bit slower. I was afraid I was tiring him out.

"I'd better go and let you get your sleep, Walter," I finally said, packing up my sketchbooks and pencils.

"Are you coming to the dinner next Sunday?" he asked. "It's just our little group here, but those of us who can, wheel out to the dining room for some visiting. I'd love to introduce you, my niece."

I slowly put my bag down beside his bed. "Of course I will, Walter. But first, I think there is something you should know."

"Hush, now, child." He put his giant, charcoal, wrinkled hand over my freckled, pale one. "Hush, now."

# Laura Koerber

Laura Koerber lives on Hartstene
Island with her husband and dogs.
A retired teacher, she works
part-time as a care provider and
volunteers at Adopt A Pet, a dog
rescue in Shelton, WA. Laura comes
to creative writing late, having spent
most of her adult life as a ceramic
sculptor and painter. Her stories
are derived from her experiences
in dog rescue combined with her
understanding of life in a region
of entrenched rural poverty.

# Ordinary Housework

Lorinda shoved the gear shift into park and killed the engine.
She sucked in her breath and exhaled loudly.

"So the plan is I go out there, wake him up, demand your dog back?"

"Yes," said Audrey, squinting at the shabby little house across
the road. The house was shut as tight as a clenched fist: windows
barricaded with cardboard, door closed. "I know she's in there. He's
asleep. Sparky sleeps until one or two in the afternoon."

Sparky, Lorinda thought. What a name for a guy who ran a meth
lab. It was hard to say how much of this was real and how much was
drama. Maybe he was just a drug dealer, not a producer. Very likely a
user, though. Audrey — tiny, disabled, wheelchair-bound lady — was
the nerve center of the neighborhood, heard all the gossip, knew all
the dirt on everyone. It was remarkable, Lorinda thought, how much
she looked like a witch: hunched over, composed of sticks and old rags,
no teeth. She knew Sparky, had known his mother and his brother, and
had gone to school a million years ago with his dad. The island was
like that; the old timers knew all about each other.

Lorinda stubbed her cigarette out and exited the car. She paused to
observe the house through the slanting drizzle. A neighbor had told
them that Audrey's missing dog was at the house. The neighbor was
a retired guy with a water view property: respectable, in other words.
Not a liar. He had seen their posters up all over the island: "Lost dog
named Chloe, border collie mix, one blue eye, one brown eye, much
loved, please call, reward."

Chloe was a dog that would not stay home. She was way too smart,
able to read human minds, able to plan a day and pursue an agenda
of her own. She knew everyone in the area, too. Her daily routine
included a ten mile circuit of visits to neighboring humans, dogs,
and horses, followed by a swim in the ocean. She came home filthy

every day. Audrey's response was to towel her off, feed her a big meal, and let her sleep off her adventures in Audrey's bed.

Lorinda ducked down to the window. "I'm going to go around back and see if she's there."

"Stay away from that barn back there. That's where he cooks his meth."

"Okay." Lorinda sprinted across the featureless front yard, hunkered over as if that would make her less visible. This is idiotic, she thought. Here I am trespassing. He could have a gun. I'm too old for this. She slowed as she rounded the corner to the side yard. Feeling a bit safer, she tiptoed along the side of the house to the back corner where she stopped and crouched. Her breathing was out of control, ragged and uneven, and sweat was popping out all over her face. She had the kind of skin that flamed at the least provocation; she knew her face was as red as the flashers on a cop car. Lorinda wiped the sweat out of her eyes with her sleeve and peeked around the corner.

There wasn't much to the backyard, just a shaggy overgrown lawn and a collapsing wire fence. Behind the fence the alders and maples jostled for space with the slick, wet huckleberry bushes. There was no dog house. There was no chain, no bowls for food and water, no dog.

Lorinda sat back on her heels. Chloe was not there. The rescue would not be easy. She wanted a cigarette. The barn?

Chloe could be in the barn. Lorinda glanced back: she could see the car parked across the road. Audrey was harder to see, her head barely visible above the bottom of the window. Was it safe to leave her sitting there? Maybe if Sparky looked out he would associate the parked car with the house across the road. It was the only other house nearby. They were half a mile as a crow would fly from Audrey's place, but a mile by gravel road uphill though the woods from the main road. Most of the area was covered by second growth forest, commercial timberlands. Any car parked along the road was conspicuous, except in hunting season. Well, she had no choice but to leave Audrey there. The whole ridiculous venture was Audrey's idea and there was no way she would have agreed to stay home.

So Lorinda had to either bag the whole project, or leave Audrey out on the road. Lorinda peered through the woods toward where the barn was reputed to be. She'd have to be fast, check out the barn quickly. There was a trail; she could see the opening in the fence, a place where the grass was worn down to mud. Could she do it? Could she run out into the open of the backyard? Lorinda took a deep breath and scampered across the stubbly grass.

She nearly fell skidding through the mud puddle at the entrance of the trail. Wet branches slapped her thighs as she ran. Her belly bounced and the flab on the back of her arms flapped, reminding her that she was too fat for this kind of adventure. She slowed to a knee-jarring trot when she got far enough down the trail to be out of sight of the house. At the bottom of the hill she stumbled to a halt. There, propped up against a Doug fir, panting, she took a quick look back up the trail; no one chasing her, no one fixing to shoot her.

She checked out the view ahead. She could just see the barn through the screen of branches and bramble. It was really just a large shack, siding gray with age, mossy roof, with one broken window in front and a closed door. Okay then, she thought. Making progress here. Time to get this over with.

Lorinda negotiated the remains of the trail carefully, trying hopelessly to fend off wet branches. She halted at the edge of the woods and sniffed. Weren't meth labs supposed to really stink? She could smell the moss and leaves, a bit of salt from the bay, and the underlying dankness of wet dirt, but nothing unnatural, nothing toxic and man-made. But she'd better be careful. There might be a lab there and that meant booby traps. Lorinda leaned around a tree for a better look.

The shack slumped in a small clearing. To the right an old road, nearly overgrown, lead down a gentle slope toward the water. Maybe at one time the shack had housed a car or a tractor, but now it didn't look watertight. Lorinda gathered up her courage for a final approach across the grass to the door.

It was the original door, solid wood, weathered to silver, the kind of door people paid big money for to hang on their summer homes for the authentic rustic look. She stood by the door, thinking of stories she'd heard of doors connected to shotguns or explosives, devices to maim intruders. It was probably locked anyway. Then she remembered that if Chloe was inside, she'd bark. Sparky up at the house wouldn't hear her knocking or hear any dog responses. She raised her arm and took two hard shots at the door.

Nothing. Chloe wouldn't sleep through that. But maybe the knocks just woke her up, but weren't enough to make her bark. Lorinda banged two more times.

No sound. Chloe was not there.

What a relief. She wouldn't have to break in. But now Lorinda was curious. Was it really a meth lab or was that just a rumor? Lorinda stepped sideways to the window and stood on tip toe.

In the dim gray interior it was hard to distinguish one item of junk from another. With an effort she picked out a lawnmower under a snarled up pile of garden hose. One corner was a thicket of long handled garden tools. But opposite from the window, on a built-in wooden work table, glass vials and bottles gleamed dully in the half-light. Metal trays, too. And a row of round, metal containers squatted sullenly in the dust.

Oh, my gosh, it was a lab! She stepped back quickly and retreated in a scurry to the trees. It was a lab! Right there in the shack where half the local old timers knew about it. Suddenly Sparky no longer seemed like an evil malignant drug dealer: more like a recklessly stupid one, so dumb he was sound asleep while a trespasser discovered his lab.

She had to get out of there. Lorinda retreated quickly up the trail, jumping around mud puddles even though she was already soaked beyond redemption. She couldn't wait to tell Audrey that the gossip was true. They'd have to call the police. But she still needed to get Chloe and Chloe must be in the house.

Adrenaline powered her climb back up the hill, but she disciplined herself to slow as she approached the end of the trail. Lorinda hunkered down for the final approach and peeked at the back of Sparky's house. Still no sign that he was awake. There were three windows overlooking his backyard: a little one, probably the bathroom, with the blinds drawn and two larger ones, probably bedrooms, both covered, one with a blanket printed with a Confederate flag. Yeah, Sparky was an asshole.

So it was safe to skedaddle. Lorinda sprinted across Sparky's yard and up to the front corner of his house. She checked the car; only the gray fuzz on the top of Audrey's head was visible. Audrey was hiding, or maybe asleep. Lorinda had a moment of exasperation, thinking of

Audrey snoozing while she ran around scaring the crap out of herself. But she wasn't done yet. She had to confront Sparky.

Lorinda marched up to the front door. It was a measly little box of a house, painted a garish light green, with concrete blocks for front steps. The door was cheap plywood. Lorinda got ready to knock.

She thought, I look a sight. All bedraggled. She brushed her wet hair back from her face, and knocked politely on the door

No sound.

Okay, polite would not work. She took her fist and hit the door hard three times. Was that a yelp from the interior? Chloe! Her heart jumped.

"Holler at him!" Audrey yelled from the car.

Oh, she's awake now, Lorinda thought.

"Holler at him! Tell him to get his ass out of bed and answer the door!"

Like she was going to do that! Instead Lorinda balled up her fist and thumped three more times. "Hey, Sparky," she called, and listened again.

Footsteps. Suddenly the door was thrust open. Lorinda jumped back to get out of the way. A tiny skinny guy stared out, barefoot and bare-chested in low-rider jeans slung so low she could see curly crotch hairs above his belt buckle. He looked groggy, but also looked like he was exaggerating the grogginess.

"What the heck?" he mumbled, eyes barely open. "Whadayou want?"

"I'm here to get Audrey's dog. You need to give her dog back."

"Don't have no dog in here." There was a jeering tone to his voice as if he was challenging her to disbelieve him. He had the dog all right, but he wasn't going to give her back.

"The neighbors saw her in your yard, chained up. You need to give her back," Lorinda could hear her voice wobbling.

Sparky could heard it too, "I don't have no freakin' dog. Get off my porch and outa my yard."

Something — maybe the way the ugly little weasel stared at her breasts, or maybe the way he started to close the door before he had even finished his sentence — lit a fire in Lorinda. She grabbed the door, jammed her thigh against it, and hissed with wrath. "I know you have a meth lab in your barn, and if the dog isn't back home in fifteen minutes the cops will be here! You got that?"

Sparky staggered back a step, babbling something that Lorinda was too upset to understand. She leaned forward, stared into his face and slammed her words into his eyes. "Give her back. You got that?"

Then she let go of the door, spun on her heal, and stomped across the yard to the car. She felt electrified, as if lightning bolts were shooting out her fingers. Audrey greeted her with a cackle, "I heard you! I heard you tell him!"

Lorinda slammed the car door and jammed the key in the lock. Sparky was gone, back in his lair. She checked the time on the dashboard clock: just twenty or so minutes short of three.

It took four minutes to get back to Audrey's house. It took another eight to haul her wheel chair out to the car, pry Audrey out of the car seat, plop her on to the wheel chair, and wheel her back up the ramp into her house. Lorinda parked her in her favorite spot, halfway between the TV and the window, next to the coffee table and the telephone. They'd left a set of wet wheel tracks on Audrey's worn carpet. Lorinda frowned at the mud, but she knew Audrey didn't care; most of her furnishings were tired and dirty. Lorinda didn't sit down; her nerves were snapping with excess energy. She wanted a cigarette.

"He's almost out of time," she said. An ugly antique clock squatted on the mantle.

"Give him five more." Audrey grinned malevolently. "Scared him, you did. I saw his face."

Lorinda thought maybe he didn't have Chloe. Maybe all that drama had been for nothing. She looked around the crowded shabby room, realizing that she hadn't done any work for Audrey that day. The dishes weren't washed. Audrey wasn't washed. The housework wasn't done. Her shift was two hours long, and most of it was gone.

"Audrey, can I get you anything? Some soup?" Audrey lived on Top Ramen and mushroom soup from the food bank. Lorinda tried to sneak canned beans or peas into the soup sometimes to get something green into Audrey.

"Naw, I'm fine." Audrey had her ear cocked, listening. For an old lady she had great hearing. Good eyes, too.

"What's that?"

Lorinda turned toward the door. A scratching sound.

Oh, my gosh! She was at the door in two big steps and flung it open. Chloe pranced in, her beautiful tail aloft. She ran straight to Audrey, crying and squealing, wriggling her whole body with joy. Audrey held out her skinny arms and cradled Chloe's face with her spidery old fingers.

"There now," she crooned. "There now, don't make a fuss." She looked up at Lorinda, tears glittering on the papery skin of her cheeks.

Lorinda collapsed onto one of the plastic kitchen chairs, suddenly exhausted. She wiped her face on her sleeve, and shoved her wet hair back behind her ears.

"Well, I'm glad that's over with." It didn't seem real now, her adventure with the drug dealer. She was forty-three years old. Running around in the woods, yelling at people, getting soaking wet, this was not normal for her. The old mantle clock chimed three ringing tones.

"Oh, my gosh, I'm supposed to clock out already." Lorinda grabbed her tote bag and extracted a pen and her time sheet. She hadn't done anything on the care plan. She couldn't mark "Cooking, Eating, Dressing, Personal Hygiene, or Shopping." She hadn't even had time to bring in some wood. Lorinda glanced up to ask Audrey what to mark, but Audrey was poking her TV remote with her toothpick fingers, channel surfing with the sound off, and Chloe was sprawled on the floor at her feet. They were entirely back to normal, as if nothing had happened. Lorinda's pen hovered over her time sheet. Then, thinking "ok, whatever," she marked the line for "Ordinary Housework."

# Edward Marcus

---

Edward Marcus is an author, composer, and website developer. Along with several short stories, he has produced two novels, available as e-books: *Money Talks* and *A Wondrous Thing*. *Money Talks* is also available as an audiobook, narrated by the author.

Mr. Marcus began his writing career many years ago, as a member of a technical-writing staff producing computer software instruction manuals. He has started writing fiction only rather recently (despite his observation that most computer manuals seem to contain at least a line or two of fiction).

Mr. Marcus's musical compositions have been performed by the Chroma Chamber Orchestra Chicago, the Seattle Symphony, Orchestra Nova San Diego, the Sidney Classical Orchestra (British Columbia), the Utica Symphony Orchestra, and the Catskill Symphony Orchestra, among others. He has taught music theory and composition at Hamline University and Concordia University in St. Paul, Minnesota.

Mr. Marcus lives in Packwood with his wife, Penny.

# *What On Fleem*

1.

Why is it, wondered Plajnikka Xarc, that every damn science fiction
story he had to read took place in space?

Well, not quite every one, he admitted to himself. There was
the occasional post-apocalyptic screed. A few stories involving
underground civilizations had crossed his desk. And once in a red
moon someone would come up with something new about robots,
and even set the story on good old planet Fleem for a change.

But all the other tales took place in space. Somehow most aspiring
writers seemed to think that all they had to do was write a regular story,
throw in some stars and a sleek metal spaceship, and — presto! — they
were writing science fiction. For the love of Oof, Xarc thought, can't
people be even a little imaginative?

Xarc rubbed the spot on his left tentacle he had bruised in the
company hairball game over the weekend. This felt good, not only
because rubbing the spot relieved the pain, but because it brought
back the memory of how he had gushed into third base on that close
play. Xarc had never been much of an athlete, and he still reveled in the
success of the play and the surprised appreciation of his teammates.

Xarc glanced at his watch. Two more hours, he realized grimly. Half
a workday left. The time would go faster if something worthwhile
would pop up, something just a little original and interesting from this
stack of submissions. Where were this generation's new voices? Who
would fill the void left by the old masters? Carbfil Geez was gone;
Plepnep Hy Fiznup was an old woman in a nursing home; and Sarb
vun Habb, though still in his 130's, had ruined his livers with too many
methane cocktails over the years and was no longer able to write. Xarc's
front eyes still teared up at the thought of this terrible waste of talent.

Xarc oozed slowly around his office for a few minutes, just staring at
the walls and trying to calm himself down. Yes, he was frustrated with

how things were going, but he also had to consider himself fortunate. There were not all that many jobs available to recent Briggish majors. Many of his fellow graduates were still looking for work, two years out from obtaining their diplomas. The recent resurgence of interest in science fiction had helped provide Xarc with an opportunity. Xarc had married right out of school, and that, combined with his naturally strong desire to earn a living, had convinced him to put aside lofty and esoteric literary dreams, for a time, and apprentice as an editor for *Bleak Vacuum* Magazine.

"Break's over," Xarc said out loud, allowing himself just one more moment of recalled glory at his great success in yesterday's game. He sat back down on his chairs behind his desk, adjusted the left one to make his tentacle more comfortable, and pulled another manuscript from the pile.

"Space To Relax," this one was titled. Xarc sighed softly through one of his left ears. Now, now, he told himself. It's just the title. Maybe this one isn't an outer space story. Xarc toyed with the idea of putting on his front glasses. He had bought them, as a joke, when he got the job. He thought they made him look busy and studious, and would make a good impression whenever his boss walked in. But Xarc's boss had gone home for the day.

Xarc kept an open mind about the story for about three minutes. This was all it took to scan the first half of it, which was even less creative than he had feared. After the fourth use of the phrase "inky blackness," he tossed the pages onto his desk and stared off into what he hoped was anything but space.

Xarc could readily understand the fascination with the unimaginable distances and emptiness that surrounded the world. There was probably no better way, and certainly no easier way, to take a reader away from the pedestrian and familiar than to set a story in outer space. Add a few alien creatures, and by definition you have transcended the reader's experience.

No one on Fleem had any way of knowing whether any other worlds harbored life, beyond the few spores and microorganisms that had been discovered on nearby planets. Certainly no contact had ever been made through radio waves or other transmissions from other solar systems. Xarc suspected that, even if the universe was teeming with advanced life forms, they all shared this same sense of isolation. Distances were so unthinkably vast, he felt, and pockets of life so vanishingly small in comparison, that most planetary civilizations must wonder if they are alone, even if they dream hopefully that they are not.

Maybe all these submissions to the magazine were not just simplistic grabs at easy science fiction writing. Maybe they betrayed a deep yearning on the part of people who thought about these things, a wish to know, once and for all, that we are not alone, maybe not even particularly special.

Xarc shook his heads. Could he really be so arrogant as to think he knew other people's deepest thoughts and hopes? He barely knew his own. Philosophizing was getting him nowhere, though he noted with some satisfaction that he had eaten up nearly half an hour since he last glanced at his watch.

Xarc concentrated on his work for the rest of the allotted time, and placed the least hackneyed stories in a small pile to be sent for further review. He looked out the window. The weather was fine, and the indoor/outdoor thermometer showed it was a bracing 125 degrees outside. He would ooze home today and save the cab fare.

## 2.

The house was empty when Xarc returned home that afternoon. He washed his hands, dried them all on some towels, and opened the food case. Often his wife left him something for second lunch when she was out.

Xarc corralled some items for his meal and put them in a food net. Their excited racing inside the net made him salivate. It had been a long time since first lunch. It was odd there was so much food in the case, thought Xarc. Then he remembered his wife would be staying overnight at her mother's house. She had left extra food for him. Xarc would be alone for the evening.

Xarc hated being by himself in the house. He brought his second lunch to the dining table, along with a food swatter, and sat in front of the tube while he ate. The tube was about two feet in diameter and was hooked up to the heating system. Xarc enjoyed the warm draft it gave off.

After second lunch, Xarc read for a while. The reading he did at home was much different from the manuscripts he had to review at work. He read some sports articles, just to relax, and then began to reread a literary classic he had first encountered in his youth. He still clung to the hope that he could make professional use of his knowledge of the classics. He wasn't quite sure how, other than teaching, and Xarc wasn't really fond of teaching.

First dinnertime approached, but Xarc had eaten so much at second lunch he wasn't really hungry. He closed his eyes, front and back, and drifted off to sleep.

3.

When the aliens came, it was not in any of the ways usually found in science fiction. There was no spaceship. There were no lights or odd sounds. There was no sudden wind.

They rang the doorbell.

Xarc awoke, but he felt groggy. He wasn't used to sleeping during the day, and he was disoriented at first. Had he heard the doorbell, or did he dream it?

The doorbell sounded again. A shot of adrenaline coursed through Xarc's system. It was rare for anyone to come to the door of his home, especially this late in the day. Xarc wondered if he should clear the remains of his second lunch before possibly having a visitor inside the house, but whoever was there had already rung twice. He didn't want his visitor to go away.

Xarc flowed quickly to the door. He scraped his skin against a piece of furniture in his haste, and the pain made him hiss a swear. Fully awake now, he interrupted the lock field on the front door with a tentacle. The door slid open.

A surprising sight might have caused Xarc to gasp. An unbelievable one might have caused him to faint. But the figures at Xarc's door were incomprehensible in his experience. He was capable only of freezing and staring.

"Mr. Plajnikka Xarc, we have traveled a long way to see you." There were six creatures, of some sort, at Xarc's doorway. Xarc slowly shifted his stare to one of the two creatures in front. He was fairly certain this was the one that had spoken. He was less sure from what orifice or area the voice had emanated. It was a low voice, but pleasant, almost beautiful.

Xarc was not nearly capable of saying anything yet, and didn't.

"We know you must be overwhelmed to see us, and hope the shock will not do you any lasting harm. We couldn't figure out a way of avoiding such a surprise."

Maybe the flaccid, cabbage-leaf-like portion in the bottom middle, thought Xarc. Maybe that's where the voice is coming from. He wet himself.

"Perhaps it would do you some good to sit down," continued the voice gamely, sounding a little concerned. "We could come into your abode, if you are willing to invite us."

Their skin, if skin it was, was shiny and jet black. It might have been damp. Xarc was not eager to find out.

Xarc sat down. There were no chairs beneath him, so the maneuver was not particularly successful. The aliens considered helping him up from the floor, but correctly feared that a move in Xarc's direction would only make his unease worse.

"We can come back later, if you like," said the alien doubtfully.

"No!" said Xarc. "I mean," he added, realizing he had sounded rude, "no, don't come back. I mean," he tried again, "you don't have to leave. Unless you want to. Don't leave unless you want to. Am I on the floor?"

"Yes, you are," said the alien. His voice was soothing. "Would you like to be not on the floor?"

Xarc thought about this. He considered all the angles. If he got up, he might have trouble standing again, and the first trip downward had hurt. But he felt compromised down here. He felt it just wasn't right.

Xarc's minds had by this time processed the situation with some success. The presence of the visitors was no longer incomprehensible to him, just unbelievable. This improvement allowed him to put off any decision about getting up off the floor. He fainted.

4.

"Should we come back later?" said Guu to the group.

"I don't know," BuuLog offered. "He's more fragile than we figured."

"He's breathing, isn't he?" Taa pushed forward a little to check, and realized there was no way to be sure what breathing looked like on a Fleemer.

All of the aliens stared at Xarc, sprawled stickily on the floor, for several minutes.

"Should we come back later?" Guu asked again. The long trip had taken the edge off their decision-making capabilities. The group stared for a minute or two longer, and then Xarc stirred. He opened his back eyes.

"Hello," he said. "I'm glad you're still here. I just needed to rest up a bit. Would you like," he said amiably from the prone position, "to come in?"

The alien creatures gave Xarc plenty of clearance as they maneuvered themselves around him. Even while viewing them from his vantage point on the floor, Xarc was not certain how the creatures moved from place to place. He assumed an upright stance and followed his guests into the living room. It was crowded in there.

"Do you sit?" he asked, and suddenly felt that sounded too inquisitive. "That is, would you like to sit down?" he corrected himself.

"Thank you, no," responded Taa. "We will lean, if that is all right."

"Of course," replied Xarc. And they did. There was quiet for what seemed to Xarc like a long time. Finally he addressed the tilted aliens. "Is there, uh, something I can do for you?"

"You would probably like to know why we are here," Guu offered. "If you find it pleasant, you may guess and we will tell you if you are close."

A flood of science fiction stories jostled for position in Xarc's mind. He had read what seemed like every conceivable reason an alien civilization might take to their spaceships and visit another planet. He really did not want to play a guessing game, but even more he did not want to insult the creatures in his living room.

"You have an insatiable urge for exploration," Xarc tried, "and your travels have eventually and accidentally brought you here."

"No, Mr. Xarc, that is a lovely thought. But that is not it," said Guu.

"You know me by name."

Guu smiled amiably, though Xarc had no idea that Guu's slight rearrangement of features represented anything in particular.

"Yes, we do, sir."

"Great. That's nice."

"Would you like to keep guessing?" Xarc was asked.

What the hell, thought Xarc. He mentally paged through more of the plots behind the stories he had read.

"You are running out of something, and are hoping to find what you need on another planet. You are running," Xarc specified, "out of water."

"We are running out of something, Mr. Xarc, but it is not water."

"Women, then," suggested Xarc. "You are running out of women."

The creatures looked at each other. Guu answered. "We are women, Mr. Xarc." Xarc thought he detected an insulted inflection. "Oh, ah…" Xarc temporized. "Well, don't worry about it," said Guu finally. "It is quite understandable, I suppose. Actually, though, your answer is quite close to the reason we are here."

Xarc puckered. If their planet was running out of men, he did not want to be part of the solution.

"We are running out of something on our planet, Mr. Xarc," BuuLog informed him. "We have come to you because we think you can help us. We are a creative race, Mr. Xarc, and have a rich heritage of thought-provoking entertainments that our authors have produced throughout centuries.

"But the creative well is running dry on our planet, Mr. Xarc, and the situation has become so serious we have invested a great deal of effort to find someone who can help us. We have run out of something, Mr. Xarc, a precious resource. We have run out of ideas."

5.

Xarc sat down on a couple of his easy chairs. Faint stirrings of ego began to dispel the massive sense of unreality swirling in his head. "You have come to me for ideas? For creative ideas?"

"Yes, that is right," BuuLog replied. "One major interest we have long had in our culture is science fiction, and our best creative minds are currently at a standstill."

"Then you know what I do for a living."

"Yes, we do. That is why we have come to you."

Xarc smiled now. "Out of all the people who do my job, you have selected me?" Xarc's hearts swelled with pride. To be noticed by an alien civilization, selected individually for his expertise in their time of dire need!

"Yes, Mr. Xarc, out of all those people."

"Why me?" Xarc asked. He felt a wave of expansive generosity toward the other, less gifted members of his important profession.

"After all, there are other editors that have been at their jobs longer than I. Of course, they might not be as talented, have the same insight, the same ability to quickly grasp the worthiness of a concept, determine whether a storyline has been well executed —"

"At random, Mr. Xarc."

Xarc crashed dizzily back to Fleem. "Oh?"

"Yes. We have no way to tell who is good at your job, Mr. Xarc. After all, if we had that kind of skill on our planet, we wouldn't need you."

Xarc tried to stoke the embers of his vanishing compliment. "So, was there a qualifying round, any effort at all to narrow the field?" he asked.

"No," replied Guu. "We threw a dart."

"Ah."

"We hit you with it."

"I've got it," confirmed Xarc.

"And now, we are hoping you will help us," finished BuuLog. Xarc had another sudden fright. In every science fiction story he had read involving aliens, "help us" meant "come with us." Xarc felt quite outnumbered in his living room. It had been foolish to let these creatures in.

"But I don't want to go. I like it here," said Xarc. His voice was high and pinched.

"Go?" replied Guu. "You mean, go back with us? No, of course not. We're not trying to abduct you, Mr. Xarc. We're just trying to make use of your expertise. If you could provide us with some ideas to take back with us, or maybe some new ways of thinking that we can explain to our creative types, we will take them back to Gerk and disseminate them. Of course, we are quite willing to reimburse you for your time and effort."

"How would you pay me?" Xarc asked.

Guu considered this for a while. "Well, I suppose our currency would be of no use to you. And you are clearly not interested in sex with us."

"I —well, it's just —"

"No, that's okay. There are planets where we are considered quite attractive."

"Oh, I have no doubt."

"Quite attractive indeed."

"Yes, I can certainly see —"

"You're no great catch yourself, you know."

"Well, sure." Xarc felt the conversation slipping away. "Don't worry about paying me. The thrill of helping another civilization with its creative problems certainly will be reward enough." Xarc hoped for some sort of argument on this score.

"Okay," replied Guu.

"Truly, it's an honor," pressed Xarc.

"Great," said Guu. "We will say no more about payment. So what sorts of things do you have in mind?"

Xarc oozed slowly around the room, thinking. Maybe it was the presence of the aliens, or the shock he was still undergoing, but his brain seemed slow and ineffective. For years he had bemoaned the lack of creativity and originality displayed by the authors of the submissions he read for a living. He had always assumed that he could do better. But now, pressed to actually come up with fresh ideas, his creative machinery was curiously inert.

BuuLog helped him. "Mr. Xarc, since you don't know what ideas we have used in our culture, perhaps you could simply express some thoughts. It is possible, I suppose, that a concept you consider overdone has not been explored in our society."

"Okay," said Xarc, his mind clearing a bit. "How about robots? Have you had stories involving robots?"

BuuLog looked at the others. "I'm afraid so, Mr. Xarc, to the point of exhaustion. But please keep going."

Xarc tried again. "Underground civilizations? You know, people living under the surface of your planet?"

"That is where we do live, Mr. Xarc, but your point is well taken. Unfortunately, fiction about surface dwellers has been quite commonplace for many years."

Xarc found his mind working gradually better, and he offered ideas that had occurred to him in the course of his tenure at *Bleak Vacuum*. None of them were original to the aliens in front of him. He was profoundly depressed to discover that a dearth of new creative storylines was such a widespread problem.

At length, Xarc shook his heads. "I'm not sure I can help you. I wish I could give you some ideas from the manuscripts I have read at work, but almost all of them are about things happening in space. You know, the same old tired stories on spaceships."

The aliens, who had been comfortably leaning all this time, stood upright.

"Space? You mean actual travel in space?" BuuLog's voice sounded different.

"Yes," replied Xarc, confused. "You know, the way you got here."

The creatures laughed, though to Xarc it merely sounded like sheep doing crossword puzzles. "No, Mr. Xarc, of course we didn't travel in space. Real space is much too big. We would never get anywhere if we traveled in space."

"Then how did you get here?"

"Well, on the subway, of course."

"The subway?"

"Mr. Xarc, are you saying you do not know of the subway? The series of interconnected travel paths between the major solar systems, with the moving portals that stop at the planets?"

"No! That's amazing. Did you build it?"

There were sheep-and-pencil sounds again. "Oh, no, of course not. It's just always been there. It must have been built very long ago by some sort of clever civilization. It probably involves wormholes, or something. We just use it."

Xarc marveled.

"But you say there are stories about traveling in space?" BuuLog continued.

"Well, yes, hundreds of them," replied Xarc. "Our writers here seem to think all you need is a spaceship —"

"Excuse me, Mr. Xarc," interrupted Guu. "A 'spaceship?' You mean, a water-bound conveyance moving in some fashion outside the confines of the subway?"

"I mean a craft, or powered enclosure, that travels in space, carrying people, food, fuel, and other supplies." Xarc paused, still in disbelief. "You really don't know about spaceships?" he asked.

"No, indeed," said Guu. She had taken out some sort of pad and was making notes. Xarc tried not to speculate about where she had been hiding the pad, or the writing implement. None of the aliens seemed to be wearing clothes.

Xarc began to recite cliche after cliche in a sort of cathartic stream. "Yes," he said, "a spaceship wings its way through the inky blackness of space, the endless void. Planets and stars wink and blink like jewels in the jet-black vacuum. The metal of the spacecraft, sleek and glistening in the fire of starlight, provides a stellar backdrop for romance in the depths of the cosmos." Xarc nearly gagged at the recitation of hoary old phrases, but the aliens were entranced.

"Hold on, hold on," said Guu, who was writing furiously. "Sleek... stellar... depths of the cosmos. This is wonderful, Mr. Xarc! Wonderful!"

"I'm glad you think so," Xarc replied.

"These rich ideas will keep our authors occupied for many, many years to come. Mr. Xarc, we are grateful to you."

"Oh, well, it was my pleasure."

"Very grateful."

"It is my honor to serve."

"Very, very grateful, Mr. Xarc," said Guu mellifluously, as she edged closer. She rested her head playfully next to one of his. "I would still like to see you rewarded for your efforts. You and I could go upstairs and —"

"My wife will be home soon!" Xarc said with sudden inspiration. He looked ostentatiously at his watch. "Any minute!"

Guu moved away. "You're married? I didn't know, Mr. Xarc. I do apologize."

"Oh, well, that's okay."

"Your wife is a lucky woman, if in fact she is a woman."

"She is. She is."

BuuLog cleared something in her vocal area. "Guu, if we leave now we can catch an early transport," she said. She was looking at some sort of device she was holding in what Xarc assumed was a hand. "The portal detector says there will be an opening nearby in about twenty minutes."

Xarc had a sudden thought. "Perhaps in exchange for what I've done for you, you could describe how we can use the subway!"

"We'd love to, Mr. Xarc," said BuuLog, "but we haven't a clue how it all works. The detectors were left on our planet by someone, and we're not allowed to give any away. We would be in big trouble if we returned without this one. Don't worry, when your society reaches a sufficient level of sophistication, you will develop the necessary skills to find and use this amazing resource. Or," she said, "you could just get really lucky, like we did. Well, we'd better be off."

Xarc watched with mixed emotions as the aliens departed. On one tentacle, he was relieved that the highly stressful events of the day had come to a close. On the other tentacle, he was profoundly relieved he had escaped whatever physical encounter Guu had had in mind.

Xarc slept well that night, and approached his work the next morning with new-found energy and optimism. For he alone on his planet knew there was another civilization out among the stars. He alone knew that one day, when science on his planet caught up with the strange wonder the aliens had told him about, his children or his children's children would be able to travel to distant planets.

He hoped the discovery of the portals would come within his lifetime. Xarc promised himself that on that very special day, if he were still among the living, he would collect all the space stories he had rejected on this job and send them into the wormhole. Now he knew that somewhere out in the inky blackness of space, in the endless void glittering with stars like jewels, there was a reader for every writer; a match made in heaven.

# SUZANNE STAPLES

Suzanne Staples is a native of the Pacific Northwest and a life-long birder. She has spent time birding in the Americas and Europe as well as in her backyard.

She writes her observations in a regular column, "Northwest Nature Log", for the *Chinook Observer*, the Long Beach Peninsula newspaper.

Travel pieces have been published in *Bird Watchers' Digest*, and poetry in *Manzanita Quarterly, Verseweavers* (anthology of the Oregon State Poetry Association) and the *Astoria Review*.

Suzanne lives and writes in Ocean Park, Washington.

# The Prince Phillip Hotel

"Well, speak up, please. Do you know this wine or not? Is there someone else whom I can speak to about this wine?" Holding the parchment wine list, John twisted in his chair to look up at the silent, smiling black woman. Like most of the hotel staff, she was from one of the Amerindian villages near Georgetown. Not more than nineteen, tall and statuesque, she had luminous eyes and black hair pulled tightly into a bun at the back of her neck. The waitress continued to smile silently as she backed away from the table. The rest of us around the table had either buried our heads in our menus or were staring at John in pained amazement.

"Really, John, you're in the third world. You can't expect a native woman just in from the bush to discuss a Chateau Neuf du Pape with you. Give her a break." This came from Mel, one of the older men in our birding group.

"If they have a Chateau Neuf on the wine list, then they'd damn well better have someone who can tell me if it's still good. Oh, what the hell." John turned again in his chair and motioned impatiently to the woman who waited, order book in hand, a few feet away.

"This one, please," he said, enunciating the 'please.' "We will have this wine." With exaggerated movements he pointed out a wine on the list. She nodded silently, eyes down, as she wrote in her order book, then walked away. Near the main restaurant door, the hostess, an older Asian woman, watched with narrowed eyes as the waitress retreated.

She shook her head slightly, unsmiling. When the wine arrived, the group waited tensely as the waitress skillfully removed the cork and poured a taste for John. Fortunately, the wine was acceptable and the rest of the meal passed without incident.

This was the second leg of a two-week birding trip in Guyana. Our group had returned to Georgetown from Santa Mission, an

Amerindian post deep in the bush. We had planned a three-day rest before embarking on a boat trip down the Demarara River, then cross-country by jeep to Shanklands, a resort on the shore of the Esiquibo River. While in Georgetown we planned to tour a ginger plantation and a boat ride down the Mahocany River to see howler monkeys and houtzins. The picture in *A Guide to the Birds of Venezuela*, the book most of the birders were using as a reference, described the houtzin (pronounced what-zin) as a chicken-like bird with striking bright blue feathers growing out of the head in the style of a Mohawk haircut. We couldn't wait to see them.

Georgetown, the capitol of Guyana, is a rough, rowdy city where tourists are strongly discouraged from wandering unescorted. Masked with a lush, thick garden, fortress-like walls surround the Hotel. Just outside the city, the jungle is an impenetrable mass of green. Most travel in the bush is by river; the few roads are deeply rutted and muddy.

The surrounding Amerindian villages provide staff for the big hotels and government agencies in the city. The people are dark, soft-spoken and extremely polite. Those who have been educated in the local schools speak with a delightful, slurred British accent. Their habit, when embarrassed by the behavior of others, is to smile politely and not say a word.

Our group was up with the sun the following morning. Breakfast was served in the elegant dining room where, outside the generous window, a dainty jacana, a long-legged wading bird, stepped delicately from one lotus leaf to another in the pond. He flashed brilliant yellow under-wings as he darted after small fish. Blue-gray tanagers flitted through the shrubbery and a flock of raucous, screeching parrots flew over on their way to a day of foraging in the nearby jungle. It was only seven in the morning and the temperature was already seventy-five degrees.

Our professional guide, Mike, was a veteran tropical birder. He could name most of the birds simply by hearing their songs. Cynthia and I, experienced birders from the Northwest, traveled together as often as we could afford a journey. Bill and Mel were seventy-eight-year-old native New Yorkers and lifelong friends who had birded together since grade school. They were made of shoe leather: tough, flexible and, so far, inexhaustible, telling wonderful, opinionated tales about each other. John, who'd been so rude to the waitress, was a

New Englander who let it be known that he was a Princeton grad with a law practice in New York City. He had left his wife at home so that he could enjoy 'roughing it' for a few weeks, adding to his extensive life bird list. He looked pristine that morning, as usual. A crisp seersucker shirt was tucked into creased khakis and a clean baseball cap covered his sparse light brown hair. No matter how hot and dirty the bird walks were, John seemed to stay clean and cool.

———

Mike had downplayed the safety aspect, but the group had overheard the East Indian bartender at the hotel's main bar talking about a British man who had wandered into one of the rougher parts of town and was 'chopped' for his wallet. This was the local description of a machete attack. So, rather than wander outside the walls in search of a restaurant, our group gathered again that evening at the hotel to eat and go over the day's bird list.

The same tall, young black woman was our waitress. The nametag on her maroon uniform read "Verna."

"What will you have for dinner tonight, please?" she said, starting at the end of the table farthest from John. Everyone ordered, then enjoyed reliving the discovery of a silver-beaked tanager earlier in the day. Pure black with an over-size blue-silver beak, the tanager flitted low in a cecropia tree, allowing what birders call "soul-satisfying," long looks through scopes and binoculars.

When dinner arrived, Verna and another waiter served the table. John's voice rose above the general noise of conversation in the restaurant. "Excuse me, this is not what I ordered. I ordered the baked chicken and yam soufflé. This is beef." He motioned imperiously across the table at Verna, who was still serving.

She hesitated and pulled the order book from her pocket. "Sir, I have written down what you indicated on the menu, roast beef and potato." She started to walk toward him with the open order book.

"I don't care what you wrote down, this is wrong. I don't eat beef."

Verna was still for a moment. "Yes, sir. I will bring the chicken." Verna removed the plate and with lowered eyes, moved quickly to the kitchen doors.

I leaned over and said quietly to Cynthia "I'll bet he ordered the beef. He's such a jerk, he probably just changed his mind."

"You know that 'chopping' thing the bartender was talking about? He'd be first on my list," Cynthia said from behind her napkin.

Again the hostess had watched the entire scene, her mouth formed into a tight line. She followed Verna into the kitchen and her raised voice carried through the swinging doors.

"You got her in trouble," Mike said. "She's just a kid."

"Oh, they all holler at each other all the time. Maybe it'll make her pay more attention next time," John said, sipping his drink.

Verna brought the chicken dish and quietly placed it in front of John. He didn't say thank you.

The group broke up early. We were all exhausted from the heat and humidity, both consistently in the mid-nineties. We were heading for the stairs when Cynthia suddenly pulled me aside. "Wait a minute. Come on," she said as she walked toward a small open office near the main restaurant door. The hostess sat inside, running down a list of figures, her fingers flying over an abacus.

"Excuse us, please," Cynthia said politely. She waited for the hostess to raise her eyes and acknowledge us. "Yes?" she put down the abacus and smiled.

"We," she pulled me up next to her, "want to let you know how much we enjoy the food here. It's wonderful." I nodded emphatically in agreement.

"Oh, thank you so much," the hostess said. "We are happy to give you a good experience and good food." She preened a little and fiddled with the ivory chopsticks in her pulled-back hair.

"Yes, and also, we are so taken with Verna. She is an excellent server. So attentive to our needs."

"Oh, yes? Do you think so? She is very young and I worry about her around for — uh, visitors from other countries."

"She is so polite and thoughtful. Yes, I think she's the best waitress we've had this trip. Tell her that we are very pleased. And we plan to leave her a big tip tomorrow. It's our last day." Mike had told the group that the tips were shared among staff.

"So nice to hear!" She positively glowed and relaxed in her chair. "I will tell Verna. She will be so happy."

"It's our pleasure. We know how hard it can be to get good help." At this point I pulled Cynthia gently out the door. I whispered, "Too much of a good thing, girl..."

We giggled all the way to our room.

The following day, Cynthia and I stumbled out of the early afternoon heat into the cool damp air of the hotel. The group had spent the morning not far from Georgetown on a jungle trail that led to the banks of the Demarara River. The heat and humidity had been numbing but we had seen a black nunbird. This small black bird with a very large red bill burrows nests in the ground and, if luck is with birders, can be found near rivers in Guyana. We were lucky that day.

Mike had advised the group to skip the hotel elevator unless we wanted to risk spending some very hot and airless time in it, since the power generator functioned rather intermittently. So we slowly climbed seven flights of stairs to our room. Showers and beers from the room fridge refreshed us.

The only place to rest inside and still enjoy a cool breeze was the lobby. The large marble-floored area was cool even in the heat of the afternoon. As we descended the seven flights of stairs, we heard the crunching grind of the generator shutting down. We exchanged looks but were too tired to comment on our luck. The lobby was dim and quiet. It was shaped like a cross with wide, marble floored hallways lined with small shops and offices. The central portion held the massive wood main desk and entries to the restaurant and two bars. We could hear John's laugh coming from the nearest bar where the rather ingratiating bartender regaled him with well-polished stories of unusual travelers. Along the quiet hallways, potted reddish-green banana plants with four-foot leaves reached to the skylights. Flame-like red and pink ginger blooms nodded in the breeze from the open walkways leading to the garden. We settled in rattan chairs near a trickling indoor fountain, where tiny brown birds flitted down, drank and disappeared into the surrounding ferns.

"Excuse me, would you like to see a bird nest?" The soft, familiar voice came from behind us. We turned to see Verna in the doorway of a small bookshop.

"Verna, hello," I said. "Come join us."

"I would like to show you a bird nest." Her soft accent made 'bird' sound like 'buhd.' "My brother is a gardener here. He showed me. It's just outside."

We followed her down the cool hallway into the heavy brightness and damp heat of the tropical afternoon. She walked easily ahead, stepping from stone to stone. We followed the cobbled pathway through the manicured lawn and tame roses into the back garden where the overgrown greenery looked like jungle transplanted inside the hotel walls.

"Here, this way. Please follow me exactly now," Verna said. She turned to wait then directed us carefully off the path into soft, moist soil. She pushed tree fern leaves out of her way and slowed to let us catch up. Cynthia tried to detour around an especially large and wet looking heliconia but Verna caught her arm. "No, this way. Step here." Cynthia followed.

As we pushed through a dense growth of scrubby, twisted figs, a small, brilliant green hummingbird jetted by us. We felt the turbulence from her tiny wings as she flew past. "That's an emerald hummer, Cyn — wow," I said as I turned to follow the tiny bird's flight.

"That is she. We are close to her home now. Look," Verna said. She gently lifted the side of a three-foot wide gunnera leaf to reveal a brown and gray nest suspended like a tiny hammock from the underside of the leaf. "No eggs yet, but my brother said that last year she had two babies here. She will again."

The nest could fit into a child's hand, yet it was sturdy and tight. Ingeniously built under a leathery, thorned leaf, it would protect the nestlings from rain, heat and many predators.

Verna smiled. "Isn't it lovely?" she said softly.

"Verna, this is such a gift. We would never see something like this on our own," Cynthia said as she stooped to examine the nest.

"It is my gift. You have been kind. But we should go before mother becomes anxious about us discovering her home."

Following Verna, we carefully retraced our steps back to the stone pathway. We proceeded to the cool depths of the hotel bar to celebrate our find. John was no longer there, so we shared our excitement with the Indian bartender who seemed a little surprised that a tiny green bird could cause the North Americans to be so happy. Oh well, tourists are an odd lot, his look seemed to say.

Later that evening the group gathered in the restaurant for our last dinner at the Prince Phillip Hotel. A celebration was planned because of the outstanding number and variety of species we had seen during our short stay.

"Where's John tonight?" asked Mel. We sat at our usual table in the dining room, cocktails in hand. Lunch was hours ago and we were ready to order dinner.

"He won't be joining us," Mike said. "Got himself into a bit of a fix this afternoon."

We all made appropriate murmurs of concern while burning to know if he finally ran afoul of the local community. There was plenty of trouble for an over-confident northerner to find in Georgetown.

Mike's face looked sober, but his eyes held an amused look he couldn't quite hide. "He heard a rumor about an emerald hummer nest somewhere in the back garden and tried to find it on his own. Son of a gun stepped into a nest of biting ants and they really played hell with him."

Verna stood quietly near the table with her order book in hand. She smiled and asked softly, "Will you be having wine tonight?"

Cynthia bumped my foot under the table but neither of us said a word.

—

*This story is dedicated to Marshall Tate, my intrepid traveling companion for close to thirty years.*

—

# LLYN DE DANAAN

Llyn De Danaan is an author and anthropologist.
She is a speaker with Humanities Washington. Her book,
*Katie Gale: A Coast Salish Woman's Life on Oyster Bay*
(University of Nebraska Press, 2013) has been
called "a masterpiece of creative interpretation..."
She worked for Washington Tribes, produced
curricula with Indian educators, and received the
State Historical Society's Peace and Friendship
Award. Research locations include Asia, Romania
(Fulbright Scholar), and Yakima Valley. Her Mountain
of Shell project focused on Japanese American
laborers on Oyster Bay near Olympia. She reviews
for *Choice*, the *Academic Libraries Journal*, and has
contributed to *Kithfolk*, *No Depression*, and the
Oly Mountain Boys' *White Horse* album. She was
a founding member of Mason County Historic
Preservation Commission and is a member of
Olympic Park Associates board, and a member of
South Sound Estuary Association and Great Old
Broads for Wilderness. She is emeritus faculty, The
Evergreen State College. She plays guitar and clarinet.

# Neighbors

Another early Sunday morning and he was outside somewhere near with his chainsaw. I could never sleep through its sound. It was a McCulloch 35, chipped yellow paint, something his Dad gave him he said once. "That and the title to this land, probably to get me off his back." He was proud of the saw. "One pump to prime 'er," he said. "Starts on the first pull," he added.

Time was I could tell who in the neighborhood was working on the winter wood supply by the distinct wail of each saw, every one with its slightly different screech. Oh, there were other disparities that told me who was laboring. Some saws sputter when they start. Or suddenly stall. Some must be pulled a few times and babied along to kick in. Most people were buying their wood by then. That Sunday, only one guy was at it the way this neighbor was and only one saw sounded like the McCulloch 35.

Even then, there had been lots of change since the year when I moved to the area. For example, time was you could tell who worked in the mills by counting a man's fingers when he lifted a glass for a drink. Now there's no more work in the mills. People keep their fingers. Well, most of them. In those days the local forest festival featured real "lumber jacks," the guys left over from the old days, the guys who did everything with hand tools. They knew how to roll real logs, and throw real axes, and climb snags. When the show was over, they'd roam from bar to bar in the downtown, still in their tin pants, looking for women. Then they'd bet all their money on games of liar's poker over boilermakers. That's all gone.

Now, people don't burn much wood at all. The regulations and talk of climate change and pollution eliminated most stoves. That was a loss. It smelled like Christmas outside all winter when the smoke from a dozen chimneys seasoned the air around us. We'd all be out splitting wood and dinking around cutting our kindling, feeling the chill in the air, and enjoying the sweet scent of home and hearth. There was something prideful about the outdoor work and it was satisfying to look out the window and see the wood cut and split and piled up ready. I compared my stash with everybody else's. You could judge a person's character by the size of the woodpile next to the house.

Being outside with purpose was the best part of it all. We cut and hauled our wood while watching the birds fly over and listening to the chum splashing their big old spent and battered bodies around on their way up the creek in November. We stacked our wood and caught the first glimpses of the snow clouds moving in. "I think it's gonna snow tonight," we'd tell each other gravely. Secretly, we were as excited as kids. That's gone too.

The sound of the chainsaw that Sunday rousted me out of bed earlier than I like to be up on my day of rest. How many times had I asked him to wait until at least 8? I pulled my overalls on over the tank top and waffle weave leggings I slept in and felt a hot rush of irritation as I mashed down two or three of the side snaps, flipped the straps over my shoulders, and did the clasps. I was in the flurry of a righteous anger so I didn't take time with them. I couldn't get out there fast enough. A couple of snaps in place would do to get me down the hill without my pants falling off, I thought. My blood was up so I didn't even feel the pull of the overhanging blackberries on the lane as they snatched at my arms. I ignored the sharp basalt driveway gravel poking painfully at my shoeless feet.

I spotted him wrestling the McCulloch's big blade into a round of a fallen Doug fir. He must have taken the tree down the day before because the saw hadn't been going long enough for him to do it earlier in the morning. The tree was lying over the drive where it leads to the house of the neighbor below me. She was out-of-town or there would have been a big hullabaloo over it. Her temper is sharper and quicker than mine.

His head was the first thing clearly visible to me because of an oversized yellow, red, green and black knit hat he wore all the time. It was a Rasta hat. The fellow who lived next door to me told me it was Rasta after the first time the cap appeared. "You know what that means." I didn't but was soon filled in by another slightly offended neighbor.

So there was the signature hat. I already knew who it was, of course. As I closed in on him that morning, I saw he was wearing his faded jeans. They were, as usual, held up over his skinny frame by a belt fastened on a hole he must have poked out with an awl. He had the belt cinched as tight as it would go. "A long drink of water," one of the neighbors called him.

No surprise in his outfit. It was his uniform, the hat and those jeans. He must have bought the pants long because they were always rolled up about four inches at the cuff. He was wearing a tee-shirt that had once been white from the looks of it. Now it was a dull grey and had dabs of saw oil and sap and even a little ketchup on it.

I always envied his work boots. They were rust colored leather and sewn with neat heavy cord stitching. They were no doubt waterproof. We all needed waterproof boots. What I liked best was that his boots laced up way past the ankles. They'd stabilize you and keep the rain from getting into your socks. Those boots must have been at least a size 15. He was over six feet tall so the big feet suited him.

He'd already kicked three or four stove-sized logs downhill from where he was at work. He had a bent-wheeled, splintered garden cart standing by and, near it, his grizzled hound sat at attention. She eyed me steadily and began a low growl. "Bagley," I screamed at the man to be heard over the engine noise, "Bagley! Hey, it's 6 a.m." He saw me out of the corner of his goggled eyes. He looked my scratched, angry red arms up and down and pressed the saw's off button. The dog continued to make nasty noises and tense up, waiting for a command so he could charge me. He was a well-trained dog, I had to give him that. The dog wouldn't move a muscle unless Bagley told him to.

I remember the hound when it was a handful of a pup. Bagley wanted to use it for a hunting dog and had some tricks he learned from a veteran hunter for getting it trained up. He put a piece of a rabbit he'd trapped on the end of a fish line and then he ran circles around his house with the bloody morsel trailing behind, and, behind the meat, the pup. The little hound went crazy trying to catch Bagley or the rabbit. When the animal was a year old or more and before a hunt, he'd put it in a wire cage, stop feeding it, and dangle some part of a rabbit close but out of reach to tease him. As he prepared for the hunt, he'd put the cage with the dog in the back of his pickup. When the dog was let loose and out of the cage it was crazy to catch any living thing, it was so hungry and mad.

Even when not hunting, the dog and Bagley went everywhere together. And like Bagley, the dog stayed at the house when it was home. It didn't bother the neighborhood ducks or chickens or any of us. Good thing, too, because those were times when you could shoot a dog if it wandered on to your property.

On that Sunday, Bagley told the dog to lie down and it did, but continued to stare menacingly at me. "Bagley, I've asked you so many times. Dang it." I tried to manage a little smile but I had my body planted and my back stretched taut and straight to try to look taller than I am. He gave me a crooked grin as he removed the safety glasses from his pale, bony face. It was the raw white face of a man with roots deep in the hills of Arkansas or Missouri. The glasses were cheap plastic, deeply etched on the surfaces by wear, almost impossible, I thought, to see through. "Bagley, give me a break, would ya? I gotta drive to work every other day at 5 in the morning. This is my one day to sleep in for a while." I was trying for sympathy. I wanted him to understand I worked every day and didn't depend on the government. He didn't like "freeloaders."

He looked at me, but said nothing. He slowly slid the glasses up the bridge of his nose and gave the chainsaw's rope a quick tug as he shouted over the machine's incipient roar, "It's a free country and this is my land." He was back at the Doug fir, rocking his blade back and forth and slowly making a deeper cut.

It wasn't the first time I'd had run-ins with Bagley. He scared me a bit so it took courage to say anything to him. He was a nuisance to us. He burned trash on the beach. The whole neighborhood took on the odor of the county dump when he burned and the smoke traveled up the hill and hung heavily around our houses like an unwelcome guest. He wouldn't pay his share of the road maintenance. He drove the road so fast that the dust he kicked up spoiled many an outdoor supper folks who shared the right of way tried to have in nice weather. He tapped into the community well without asking permission and when challenged produced all kinds of papers that, he said, proved he had rights to $1/15^{th}$ of the water produced by the well. We'd have to go to court to prove him wrong. And that meant hiring attorneys and that meant money. So we never got around to it. His rights didn't extend, apparently, to helping pay for upgrades to the well house and a new pump when the old one failed. He set off half an hour's worth of fireworks every Fourth of July and again on New Year's Eves. Birds and ducks left for a few days. Dogs went crazy all over the bay. Neighbors were out with hoses and rakes on the look out for flying embers and picking up papers from blown out rockets. Everyone hated Bagley.

The guy was consistent. He did what he did because, he said, he owned the land and he could do whatever he wanted on it. Not that he didn't happily encroach on other people's land. Or even government land as much as he hated the government. He was a great one for hunting mushrooms, for example, and every chanterelle season he was up in the national forest acting as if he owned it. Nobody knew exactly where he went but nobody doubted he would have murdered anyone who stumbled or crawled into "his" patch. Every time there was a shooting up in the woods anywhere in the county, we all thought of Bagley. Every time there was a report of stolen music wood from giant maples out in the national park, we thought of Bagley. Every time someone had an expensive tool go missing, we thought of Bagley. Even when our mailboxes were looted and vandalized, we thought of Bagley. Bagley was the go-to man for all evil thoughts, our fears, and our paranoia. He was our tormentor, our bogeyman, and our obsession.

Masses of auburn hair hung from his head in a misery of tangled curls when he didn't have them tucked up under his Rasta hat. I suppose he thought of those curls as dread locks. Maybe he smoked dope, we all reasoned when we talked about the hat and hair. Heck, he probably grew it somewhere up in the high places of his peculiar home. He built above the bay and put in many south-facing windows. These were placed on the highest part of the house, a strange shaped tower that rose up three slender stories. That highest story stretched above the closest trees so nothing could shadow it. We all figured, yes, he grew weed up there.

When rumors reached us that an unoccupied house down the bay had been appropriated for drug dealing, we all assumed Bagley was the ringleader. He probably ran a narcotics operation out of there, we said. "Yep, probably Bagley," people said at the mailboxes. One particularly anxious woman who lived on her own after her husband died said she had reported her guess to the sheriff. "You should all call in," she said. She even figured out his supposed route in and out of the drug headquarters. I wouldn't have been surprised if she had done a stake out on him the way those crazy people down on the Arizona-Mexico border patrol for people trying to cross into the United States. She was on his case like a pit-bull on an ankle. She had elaborate theories about Bagley's other nefarious activities she'd gladly share if anybody stood around at the mailboxes long enough to hear them.

Still, when I thought about Bagley and the house he'd built, none of it with permits and nothing to code, I thought about the magnificent view of the bay he had from way up there on the top floor. And I thought about how careful he was with his tools and how he always tucked that mess of hair into his Rasta hat and put on goggles when he used his tools. He was not a reckless man even though he was a pain in the rear end for all the rest of us.

We neighbors always wondered about his wife. She seemed as mischievous in her way as he and sometimes shouted out nasty things at us when we came too near the property line. Still there was something about her. I thought she drank but I wasn't sure. What I was sure about was she had one baby after another for a few years. Three or four. I wasn't certain because I seldom saw any of them. They all looked a lot like Bagley judging from the glimpses I had of them through her car windows when she stopped at the mailbox. They didn't make noise, those kiddies, never could be heard crying, and did not venture off their property the way some of the neighborhood kids did. Bagley's children were as well trained as his dog.

The wife was a little thing from what we could see of her. "Grew up somewhere around Marysville," I heard from one neighbor. "Used to sing in bars up there," another reported. "Likes to bake," someone said. "Gives a few piano lessons over there," someone seemed to know. And it was, I thought, true. When I listened hard, I could hear tentative tunes coming from that direction, as if there was a pair of small hands struggling to learn a keyboard.

She was a fleeting wraith. She reminded me of a dust bowl refugee. Something about her cotton dresses and the tight pin curls half covered with a scarf I'd see through her car window. The dresses were dotted with tiny flowers, made of the cotton, it seemed. It looked like the fabric that had been employed as flour sacks. Women would save the sacks, lay out patterns on them, and sew dresses and shirts from them.

She was a pretty woman with a round face and very blue eyes, and a sweet almost cupid mouth. She looked as country as a glass of cool buttermilk or a warm peach skin in the summer. However, no one made an effort to visit or talk with her after a few of her outbursts. So she was sitting there alone in her house a big part of the time… sitting there with three or four little kids while her husband was out doing the odd construction job.

Of course, we suspected the worst of that relationship. Why else would she stay in the house all the time? She was a woman you wondered about and theirs was a life we all avoided or judged or criticized depending on the day. We all figured we lived where we lived so we could sleep in on Sunday mornings and have our few acres of peace and harmony. We pretty much left each other alone. We imagined that without Bagley we'd have paradise.

A lot of what happened later, we had to piece together.

Apparently, one morning, Bagley decided to fell trees on his back acreage, the part of the forest he called his woodlot. He cut year-round to let the wood season and be ready to split for the five or six cords he used over the winter. Now Bagley wasn't too particular about property lines or fences or survey markers, so he could have been anywhere back in the woods. There were at least 50 or 60 acres of thick second and third growth forest back up the hill that we each owned a slice of. A lot of the younger stuff was alder but there were some good-sized Doug firs and some big leaf maples and some cedar and hemlock. Every one of these trees was host to something else. Moss as thick as down blankets clung to giant trunks. Lichen covered the alders' bark. Tiny sword ferns took root in the dense moss on tree limbs and even in crevasses in the Doug firs' tough exterior. Nurse trees made walking through the woods sometimes impossible. Where there were no downed limbs, the floor of the forest was a woven snare of snarly vines. There was salal and long strings of native blackberry in the mix. Tall sword ferns were so profuse as to make their own miniature forest. Rotting maple leaves and fungi that were way past their pull dates made walking springy and slippery.

We knew Bagley had been going up there to get wood for years and figuring out how to haul it out bucked up when nobody could see him. He was a stealthy character. The truth was none of us wanted to struggle up the hill and into those woods to see what he was doing so it was unlikely anybody would catch him at it. And anyway, you couldn't always hear the buzz of the saw clearly from down where the houses were. You had to strain. So you didn't know for certain when he was at it. He was pretty safe, he figured. He figured right — in a way.

Of course he had his dog with him when he went up that morning. The dog was there to warn him if anyone was coming and to keep him company, as always, I suppose.

He'd been gone from about seven, the hour when the November sky had begun to glow over the eastern hills. It was growing chilly and going on four in the afternoon when his wife thought something was wrong and began to fuss and wonder why he wasn't home. The light would be gone soon. I think it was close to Thanksgiving when this all happened. I know the chum salmon were still coming in. I remember because later we had talked about going down to the head of the bay to recruit some of those fellows who fished into late evening along the banks of the creek to come help us in the search if we didn't find him right away.

It was dark and around six when I heard the tapping at my door. By this time it was raining and the wind had come up as it does sometimes after the sun sets. The knock surprised me. I kept my doors unlocked then and almost everybody I knew just came right in calling out my name as they walked toward the kitchen. They all knew they'd find me there. It's the best place in any house. It was late for the strangers who often stopped by trying to sell meat out of a truck or hand out religious tracts or get me to invest in some tree trimming or lawn mowing. None of us cared about things like keeping our grass mowed then.

I went to the door and there was Bagley's wife. She was still in one of her lightweight cotton dresses with the tiny rosebud pattern though it must have been 40 degrees outside. She had one baby in her arms. The child was shrouded in a pink crocheted blanket from toe to the top of its head. Two slim blond kiddies were hanging on to the skirt of her dress. They were all soaked clear through. None of them had coats. The little ones were shaking. She was a little tipsy. Her words were a bit slurred and there was a hint of liquor on her breath. She said Bagley wasn't home and the fire in the big cast iron stove had gone out and this wasn't like him not to be home before dark. She seemed frightened. I got her inside and put some more wood in my stove. I found some old wool sweaters in the back closet and got the kids to put them on even though they hung well below their knees. I got everybody seated around the kitchen table while I put some water on to boil and some milk in a pan to heat. As the wife described the morning and how Bagley had gone up into the woods with the dog and chainsaw, I pushed some jars around in the fridge and found a plate of cold chicken and some lunch meat and got a loaf of bread out of the pantry. I pulled out a box of tea bags and a teapot. I put it all out on the kitchen table. The wife didn't touch any but the two little ones were hungry and went for the chicken drumsticks first.

Anything could happen to a man alone in the woods. I knew this and so did she. If he had left for the woods in the morning planning to return in the afternoon he wouldn't have had a flashlight or anything else with him. She said she occasionally caught the dull, distant sounds of his saw throughout the day, but after about two o'clock in the afternoon, she didn't hear it again. She figured he was on his way home or he had moved further back in the woods and the sound was completely muffled. Anyway, it was safe enough up there. Sometimes you'd see the full brush of a fox flagging away from you quicker than a rabbit. There were raccoons everywhere and an infrequent visitor coyote on a hunt. Nobody had seen a cougar or bobcat for years. They'd all moved away as the place went to people. It wasn't the time of the year for yellow jackets. True, in late summer they could jump out like a pack of banshees and sting you a hundred times. Even a person who isn't allergic could have a reaction or die. This time of year was too late for them plus it was dark and raining. Whatever, Bagley wasn't where he was supposed to be and the little family was frightened.

My visitors settled and warmed up. The tea had steeped long enough so I poured out a cup for the woman and refilled the pot with water, made some cocoa with the now hot milk for the little ones, and called the neighbors. At least one person if not two from every household in the neighborhood showed up at my house within ten minutes. Somebody checked Bagley's house to see if he'd come back.

He hadn't.

We all had rain gear and flashlights and a few of us had long-handled loppers and pruners and manual weed whackers so we could cut through the brush and under floor. It would be rough going as dark as it was now. There was a lot of chatting and speculating but nobody spoke ill of Bagley and nobody suggested anything that might frighten his wife and kids. We kept it light, as if we were accustomed to searching for each other in the woods every night. No big thing.

Before we set out up the hill I made the kids some more cocoa and put out a plate of chocolate chip cookies I'd baked the day before. The little girl was picking at a tear in the bright oilcloth on the kitchen table and the little boy was under the table trying to get my cat to come to him. The wife sat hunched over her cup of Lipton's looking as if she wanted to cry but couldn't. She wouldn't look me in the eye. I had given her a dark green wool shawl from a box I had ready to take to the thrift store. It had the unmistakable stink of mothballs but she had tossed it over her shoulders then crossed her arms in front of her, grabbed the ends of the shawl, and pulled it tight across her chest. She kept staring into the tea as if she might be reading the leaves (there weren't any, of course) or praying. Perhaps she was hoping some solace would rise up out of the tea's steam.

We made quite a group as we headed up the hill. We couldn't spread out the way we'd seen people do on television searches. The undergrowth was too thick and we needed to stay behind the people in our group with the whackers. We all called out in different directions and shown our lights in front of us and to the sides. One man had a compass and had brought a can of fluorescent spray paint to blaze our trail. He kept track of where we were so we wouldn't be lost or turned around up there. The fog was coming in lower or maybe we were climbing higher than we imagined. It draped itself over the hill like a wedding veil. It was difficult to see each other through it. It would be easy to get turned around. With the fog came more moisture. It covered our clothing and hair. The air licked us with such a dismal chill that we were all trembling.

We had been out about forty minutes, calling out all the while, when we saw a slight clearing up high ahead of us. You could see the quarter moon emerging from behind the clouds through the thinned canopy in that direction. We thought that could be where Bagley had been working at felling trees.

We saw him as soon as we got in under the thinning. In truth, we heard him first. It was a low growling moan and a weak "help" coming from somewhere on the ground. It was hard to see him in the dark and under all the branches and side branches and needles of the tree he had taken down. It was a big one and it lay there like a fallen colossus. Bagley appeared to be to one side of it.

If it hadn't been for his Rasta hat we might have missed him. But the yellow and green and red were unnatural colors and stood out even in those dark woods. "Bagley, damn," someone said. Another guy said, "Be careful. We've got to see what's going on before we do anything that might hurt him worse." Of course these were the days before everybody carried a phone around, so we couldn't call out for help right away. We did decide to send a couple of people back down to my house to phone the local emergency services. Not that we thought they'd get to us any faster than if we carried him out and got him in a car and took him to the hospital ourselves. We always dreaded the possibility of a fire. In those days, we knew we'd be lucky if the volunteers could find our houses.

The man with the compass gave it to one of the guys going back to call. They didn't know how to read a compass so he made sure they understood about following the blazes. The rest of us said we would either stay put until they returned or we'd head down the same trail. We were all breathing hard and confused and a little scared and uncertain what to do. I was sweating inside my rain gear. One of our group was a veteran and had done some medic training in Vietnam. He bent over and started talking in a low voice to Bagley while he looked him over. Bagley's chest and head were clear of the trunk and the big branches but a big limb had caught his legs. Both of them were pinned to the ground. The tree must have taken a bad bounce. Maybe it hit something higher up as it was falling. Bagley would have seen what was happening and tried to run. It was too late. He wasn't stupid. But you can't always tell what a tree is going to do.

The medic said, "Hand me those loppers and shine all your lights right down here." We were all happy to hand the management over to someone who had experience with these things. We were ready to obey his orders. He began cutting away at all the brush and the briars and the salal and bits of tree that restrained Bagley's head and torso. While he chopped at the brush, he continued to talk to him in a gentle whisper. "You're okay big fella. Just gotta get you out of this dang tree. We'll take care of you. Don't you worry. You'll be just fine." Things like that. Bagley couldn't see our faces but we all had silly smiles we hoped looked encouraging if he did see us. Nobody spoke of it. We shot tense looks at each other occasionally. Our eyes were too obscured in the gloom to convey much meaning but we all had an idea of what he was up against. My jaw was so taut I thought I'd break a tooth.

Bagley rasped out, "Where's my dog?" to our medic. "Where's my dog?" The medic looked up from where he crouched over Bagley and motioned for a couple of us to look for him.

I helped with that since I was of no use otherwise. We looked all around the tree and followed the length of it up and down from the stump. We saw yellow chips of paint from the McCulloch. The saw was smashed flat and buried in the ground a foot or so. Then we saw the dog. He was flattened too, like a beaver that had misjudged the angle of the tree it was falling. This happens sometimes. The poor cuss was under the trunk of the tree. Its forepaws were sticking out from one side otherwise we wouldn't have seen him at all. We surmised later he had been told to sit and stay and even when the tree was coming down on it, it wouldn't move unless Bagley told it to. But Bagley was way too busy saving himself to think about the dog. We wondered if there had been a moment, right before contact, when the dog looked real hard at Bagley in disbelief.

The medic working on Bagley looked up at us said, "We've got to get his legs free and try to get the blood circulating. We don't know how long he's been here and he is hypothermic and in shock. We've got to get him out of here." So after more pruning and cutting, we got hold of the limb that had him pinned and on the count of three lifted it as high as we could. It took a few tries to get it elevated enough to extricate him. We were careful not to let the limb fall back on his legs. Bagley stayed quiet and we continued to lift. At last, the medic and another neighbor were able together to ease Bagley out and move him free of the debris.

We were all soaked through now. Even the rain gear had become useless. But we were making progress. The medic knew how to make a gurney out of jackets so we could carry Bagley down the hill past the blaze marks and down toward my house. It was hard going but we placed two of us with flashlights up front and everybody else holding on to the rolled edges of the sling the jackets made. The flashlights penetrated a foot or two into the mist — just enough to keep us on the right trail. Bagley's legs were bloody and bleeding and looked crooked, unnatural. One of the neighbors who had gone ahead and made the call met us coming up and said an ambulance was on its way. The other guy had gone to the top of the driveway where it met the main road to wave the ambulance down and guide it to the house. Soon, we could hear the siren. Through the dark and the fog, it seemed horribly far away. The only sound we heard, apart from the distant whine was the squawk of a disgruntled heron as it departed a branch high in a madrona tree by the bank. As we came nearer my house, we could hear the engine of an oyster barge somewhere out on the mist covered bay.

We didn't see Bagley again. He had several surgeries and was in rehab, someone heard from a nurse friend who worked in the county hospital. We all carried hot dishes and sympathy cards over to the wife, but she didn't say much except thanks. After a while we almost forgot about him. Sometimes up at the mailbox someone would say they'd heard he'd gotten out of the hospital and was doing okay. The woman who had wanted to report Bagley for being a drug dealer worried he'd had his accident on her land since we didn't know where the boundaries were and he'd come back and sue her. Nothing came of that. Someone heard he was working construction in Bremerton. Someone heard somewhere he'd been sued for backing out of some contract. She couldn't remember where she'd heard that. Somebody said they'd seen one of the kids up the driveway waiting for the school bus. It could have been the week before. But then the mother must have started driving the kids to school because we never saw them up there again. One day, somebody noticed the name on Bagley's mailbox had changed. We all wondered if there'd been a divorce. Or if she had remarried. Somebody said they'd seen a pickup with an unfamiliar fellow driving it come down the lane. He pulled into her driveway. Someone said she'd heard Snyder was the wife's maiden name and that was why the name on the mailbox had changed.

It must have been four or five years passed. One early evening in June, I heard a knock at the front door. I was locking it by then, so it could have been anybody.

Things had changed a lot in the neighborhood. A couple of people had sold out and the new people seemed to think they lived on Bainbridge Island or some other upscale Seattle suburb. They built a 4000 square foot house with a swimming pool. They watched what we all did like hawks. They reported us for having burn barrels and for not having our septic tanks checked by the county. They reported one fellow to the county when they thought he was hiring illegals to cut brush. We all wished they'd leave. Meanwhile, the woman who had fussed about the drugs when Bagley was around now focused her concerns and fretting on mailbox vandalism. She called around to everyone each time she found a scrap of an envelope or a soggy flyer in the ditches along the roadside. She wanted us to call in and report. She thought it was "those young guys" who lived across the road. She was certain they'd taken a fishing rod from her car one night when she'd forgotten to lock it. The rod was later found in her own garage.

Anyway, the knock on the door. It was Bagley's wife. I asked her in but she said no she just wanted to say hello. She stood there with a look of a victorious rabbit that had outrun a hound. Proud but still twitchy. She said she remembered how nice I was the night Bagley got hurt. She wanted me to know she hadn't forgotten. She wanted to thank me, she said. She wanted me to know she was doing fine and the kids were in school and doing fine and that she had a job and was back in school part-time. She handed me a something wrapped in brown butcher paper and tied with some green garden string. I pulled at the ends of the string and opened it. There was the shawl I'd given her that night. It smelled fresh and was folded into a neat compact square. There was a bit of paper on top of the shawl. She had written "Thanks" in big block letters. Then she said as she turned to leave, "We're all fine. I just wanted you to know." And, she added, "If you ever need anything, I'm right next door."

# EVE HAMBRUCH

Eve Hambruch attended UC Berkeley where she majored in Math and English. Although she left without a degree, she did take away a love of the written word that has followed her through her life. Her knowledge of skiing and ski areas comes from her years at Mammoth Mountain, where she worked as a lift operator and later as an electrician. She lives in Glenoma, Washington with her husband of thirty-five years and two ill-mannered cats. She is currently working on her memoirs, which she intends to publish online. She is a member of WRITING FROM WITHIN, a writers' group that meets in Morton.

# Whiteout

A gust of wind swept a curtain of snow up through the chute, hiding all but the nearest tower of the chairlift. The chairs swung madly. In the lift shack, Jay banged her open palm down on the red mushroom button, certain the chair would derail this time. She held her breath as the cable slowed and then finally stopped, a chair hanger inches from the guide rail on the tower. The gust died. Jay let out the breath and buzzed the bottom station on the intercom. "Clear?"

"Who knows. It's like totally white down here. I couldn't see Bigfoot if he was making faces at me right outside the shack. Did you call Dave?"

"I called. We're probably going to shut down as soon as he checks with the patrol. Are you clear to start?"

"Yeah, I guess. Don't make any sense. Why are we keeping the stupid lift open? There hasn't been anyone through here since noon."

Jay gave him the obvious reply. "We're keeping it open because they haven't told us to shut down yet." She held down the black start button. The chair crept forward, accelerated.

The intercom squawked again. "Haven't you got anything better to do than sit here and wait for this thing to derail?"

"Yeah, I have, now that you mention it," Jay said, smiling to herself. "My kid brother, Paul, is coming up for the Christmas break. He should be here this afternoon."

"Well, why don't you give Dave another call?"

"Patience, Rob. He'll get us out of here before long. Meanwhile, didn't I see a Playboy magazine sticking out of your pack this morning? Kick back. Relax. Spend some quality time with Miss December." The bottom operator's only reply was a rude noise. Jay laughed as she hung up the intercom. She put her elbows on the windowsill and propped her chin in her cupped hands. Cold radiated from the windowpane, chilling her nose and cheeks. "Cold doesn't exist, only the absence of heat." The voice of her engineer friend sounded so real in her ears that she nearly looked behind her to make sure she was alone. Creepy. Sitting here all day with no company but the keening wind and the blowing snow made it easy to hear voices that weren't there.

Another gust whipped up the chute, and Jay slapped the stop button. The chair swung to a stop with feet to spare this time.

The phone rang.

"Top of 14. Jay speaking."

"Dave here. Hey, sorry it took so long to get back to you, but I had to chase down Hansen. He says the patrol can sweep from the top of chair three if they need to. How's the wind?"

She leaned over to look at the circular graph of the anemometer. "A gust of 62 and another of 60 just since I talked to you, and it's probably worse in the saddle."

"OK. Go ahead and shut down and get out of there." A pause. "You skiing down?"

"Yeah. I don't want to ride the chair down in this — not with no one here to watch for wind."

He hesitated. "You might think about waiting for the patrol."

"I want to get back. My brother's coming up today."

She could hear the smile in Dave's voice. "He's here right now. He says to say hi. Okay. Go ahead and ski down, but be careful."

"I will."

"You know, if you spoke to me just right, I might see my way clear to letting you have a day or so off before the Christmas rush hits. Let you get in some skiing with your brother. What would you say to that?"

She gave a little, happy jump. "I'd say, that's great. Thanks, Dave."

"Come on down now. And be careful, okay? I mean it. Stay on the cat track, and take it easy. I don't want to be out at midnight looking for you."

She smiled in amusement. The words that could have been a direct quote from her mom sounded a bit odd coming from her 28-year-old boss. "I'm always careful. I've got important things to do, remember. Just eight more credits at Fresno this summer, and I'll have my degree in Resort Management. Then I'm going to come back in the fall and take your job."

Dave laughed. "When you finish your degree in Resort Management, you'll find a lot better job than mine. Take off now, and don't forget to check in with me when you get here."

A few minutes later, standing outside the shack, looking toward the saddle, Jay was less inclined to make light of Dave's warning. Down the chairline, she could see the breakover towers, but in the other direction — the way she would have to go — a damp wind sent freezing mist swirling up the slope, concealing trees and boulders she knew were not fifty feet away. She almost wished she'd taken the chair down after all. She wasn't looking forward to the long, cold run through the exposed saddle, across the backside, past Red's lake, and around the spur to Broadway. She'd left herself no option, however. She didn't want to wait for the patrol, and the bottom operator was gone by now. She skimped on her warm-up exercises and stepped into her bindings.

A short herringbone climb took her up to the cat track. She turned and pushed off with a skating step. The low blowing snow concealed the texture of the run. Centering herself, she let her knees absorb the bumps she couldn't see. After a short descent and a single check turn, she ran into heavy mist — not quite snow, not quite fog. The damp wind sucked the heat from her body despite her heavy parka. Jay was navigating now by the loom of rocks and brush beside the trail. Her skis chattered on the corrugations left by sno-cat treads. The rushing gusts of snow at her feet made her cautious progress appear recklessly fast.

As she entered the saddle, the wind shoved her bodily sideways. She took a quick sidestep to recover her balance. A few feet later, a curtain of mist came down, swallowing vision. Everything around her was the glaring, featureless white of a movie screen when the film breaks. Vertigo seized her. She didn't know whether she was moving or standing still, balanced or falling. She made a panicky check and stopped — or thought she did. She planted her downhill pole to brace herself. Her skis crashed into it, and she tumbled in a heap. She sat up, unhurt. At least, she knew now that she was not moving.

With her nose only inches from the snow, she could see vaguely the ridged surface of the cat track. She levered herself up with her poles and set off in an ungainly snowplow, crouching down to keep her eyes close to the snow. The position was uncomfortable, but it worked. She could see well enough to keep on course and judge her speed. As long as she followed the cat track this way, she couldn't go wrong.

She found herself repeatedly nudging the left side of the trail. It took her a moment to realize this was the turn at the far side of the saddle. Here the trail straightened for the long traverse. She dared to let the tails of her skis drift closer together, picking up speed.

She thought she had seen whiteouts, but this was the real thing. She would have been terrified had she not known that she was on the right trail and that no trees or rocks were in her way. She glanced up from time to time, straining her eyes, but there was no piercing the bright, white mist. Her visible world had shrunk to the tiny patch of corrugated snow sweeping by at her feet and her skis, disappearing toward the tips.

After some time, Jay began to wonder if she had overshot the turn. Surely, the traverse was not this long. Of course, she was moving very slowly, and there was the cat track to tell her she was still on course. At last, to her relief, she heard the metallic clank of chairs as the wind swung them against the tower guide rails. She hoped it was chair 11 and that she'd passed chair 12 and Red's Lake without realizing it. She widened her skis into a broader vee and straightened, squinting in an attempt to see through the mist. Tiny ice particles cut at her eyes, bringing tears. At last, an object materialized out of the bright nothingness just at her left hand. A yellow and black striped mattress, furred by rime ice on the windward side. She blinked her eyes and looked again. Chair 11 didn't have enough fall to need mattresses to cushion its towers. If she had only reached chair 12, she was barely moving. At this rate, it would be dark before she got back to the lift crew office.

Over the worst of her vertigo now, she straightened to a more normal skiing stance. The chatter of her skis told her she was still on the trail. If she hit the berm on either side, she would know she had wandered. At the worst, she would take a fall. A fall at slow speed on such a gentle slope did not worry her.

Despite the icy blast scouring her face and cutting through her parka, she felt exhilarated. She was getting the feel of it now, learning to trust her muscles as they moved automatically to keep her in balance. She wished she dared to ski flat out, but she would never be able to stay on the trail that way. Maybe she'd get a chance to ski the cornice in these conditions sometime. On a steep run with no obstacles and no possibility of getting lost, the thrill would be fantastic.

It seemed to Jay that her hair began to prickle even before she heard the noise — a tone hovering just above hearing, then descending the scale into the audible range. The unearthly shriek faded at last into a gurgling moan. Jay's knees threatened to buckle. Her heart lurched to a standstill, and then began pounding. The sound had seemed to come from all around her, but the chill at the back of her neck said some demonic creature crouched just above her shoulders. She whipped around to look behind her, and she fell.

From her deep pit of terror, she could feel it coming after her. Its footsteps crunched in the dry snow. She didn't bother to ask herself what it was. She scrambled to her feet and poled madly to escape the menace. When she finally got control of her panic, she bent down to see if she was still on the trail. She breathed deeply with relief to see that she was. She was luckier than she deserved not to have lost herself in her blind flight. Setting off again, she admonished herself to go slowly. The sharp edge of panic overrode good intentions. It urged her to greater and greater speed. Something was out there, and it wanted her.

What was it? The sane part of her mind told her it was only a harmless coyote. Superstition, however, whispered that it was the unhallowed soul of Cooper, who had died out here last January in just such conditions as these. She shivered with more than cold.

Whatever it was, she told herself, it was behind her now. She needed to slow down. She angled her skis into a wider vee and nearly lost her balance. Much too fast. And had the trail always been this rough? She recoiled in surprise as a snow-dusted branch whipped at her face. There were no branches extending over the cat track. She had gone astray. Making a christie turn in an attempt to stop, she fell again. She levered herself to her feet, seesawing back and forth as she tried to position her invisible skis at right angles to the unseen fall line.

When she was sure she was not moving, she slid gently back and forth, prodding at the snow with her poles. The snow was packed, so she must be on a trail. It was much too narrow, however. She bent down to look at the surface, but the light was growing dim. She could see no details. Her fear came back, cramping her guts. She was lost in the midst of impenetrable whiteness with night coming on. Panic told her to flee — no matter which way — just get away from here.

Jay closed her eyes and took long, deep breaths, controlling her terror. It helped. With her eyes closed, she could trick her mind into thinking that she knew exactly where she was. She tried to visualize this area that she must have skied a hundred times. It worked. Obviously, she had strayed off the cat track and wound up on the cross-country trail to Red's Lake. The Nordic skiers were long gone, of course. By now, they were sitting in the lodge drinking hot buttered rum and soaking up the heat from the enormous fieldstone fireplace. Jay would give her new K-2's to be with them right now.

Okay. Now that she knew where she was, she only needed to follow the trail to the lodge. But could she? There were a half dozen trails out here. It was difficult to stay on the right one even when visibility was good. Only one way led to warmth and safety. Any other led to the bare sweep of ice and snow that was Red's Lake. The terrain offered no clues. The trails traversed a series of rolling hills, splitting and rejoining, crossing and recrossing. She tried to visualize the way she had come, but her fall had left her disoriented.

Jay thought again of Cooper, who had obviously made the wrong choice. A hiker had discovered his body last spring near Red's Lake. Small, easily detached parts like fingers and toes were scattered at some distance, the bones picked clean. Soft bits like nose, ears, eyes and lips had been gnawed away. The larger parts had been sampled but not consumed. A matchbook and a few burnt stubs of matches lay near the body, and his pocket still held a working butane lighter. She shivered. Not the best time to be thinking of Cooper and his blind date with hypothermia.

Jay chose a direction and set out. The trail leveled, traversing a steep slope. Her downhill gear was not well-adapted for this sort of travel. After a time, she realized she was doing exactly what Cooper must have done — exhausting herself, sweating, losing body heat. Panting, she stopped to rest. There it was again! That same satanic scream, ending in a deep, agonized groan. She didn't believe in spirits... hauntings... unnatural beings. Didn't! She had not finished assuring herself of this when she was again in panic-stricken flight. She had to get away from here. She didn't care which direction she was going, as long as it was downhill. She had to keep moving. The mist was thinner here. She could see the loom of trees in time to avoid them.

There was another inhuman moan, lower pitched this time — hopeless sounding. Just behind her, she heard snorting and snuffling followed by something that sounded like footsteps crashing through snow-covered brush. She whimpered in terror and looked back over her shoulder. She saw nothing, but that didn't mean it wasn't there.

It was upon her in an instant. The menace that she had thought was on her heels had been lying in wait ahead of her. She caught a glimpse of a thick white arm just as it reached out and snatched at her throat. She gasped and twisted away. A tree limb, the sane part of her mind told her. Before that could fully register, she was falling. Not neatly in a heap this time, but head over heels, floundering in soft snow, cartwheeling down a steep slope. Her skis were gone, her poles tangled between her legs. Her hat was lost. The neck of her parka scooped up snow. There was a blinding crash, and everything went dim.

She opened her eyes, or thought she did. She could see nothing but that glaring white light again. She blinked, clearing her eyes enough to see that she was lying in a drift. Her head hurt, but the rest of her seemed fine. She lay still a moment, gathering her strength. She ordered her body to move, to stand. No response. Her cheek and ear, pressed into the snow, were growing numb. She turned her head, but nothing else worked.

Jay closed her eyes. She would just rest for a moment, and then try again. "Guess I'll be a little late, Paul," she murmured. "Sorry." The next time she opened her eyes, it was nearly dark. She realized she must have slept — or lost consciousness. She was starting to feel comfortable. Vaguely, she realized that this was not good. She ignored the feeling. Surely it was better to be warm than to be cold.

"Guess you'll be out here at midnight looking for me after all, Dave," she muttered aloud. She laughed weakly. They'd find her all right. Like they found Cooper.

She felt a moment of profound regret. So many things she had wanted to do. She'd never get that degree in resort management now.

Never convince her father that the 'real' job he kept urging her to find was right here. She put a stop to these defeatist thoughts. 'Just keep calm,' she told herself, silently this time. 'They're out looking for you right now. Just a little nap and they'll be here.' The ski patrol would be coming with snowmobiles, a litter and blankets. Cocoa. Hot cocoa would taste so good. She'd just have a little nap, and they'd be here.

She heard again the sound of a body crashing through the underbrush, whether in reality or only in her mind, she wasn't sure any longer. Again, she tried to jerk herself erect. She cried out. Her whole body hurt, and there was a sharp pain in her right leg. No longer caring whether what was out there was friend or foe, she screamed again. Then it was on her, lapping her face with a warm tongue.

"Bear," she cried.

Dave's face loomed over her. "You scared us to death! If your brother hadn't brought your dog… I thought I told you to be careful."

The ski patrol was around her now, carefully releasing her skis from the pile of debris entangling them. They were hurting her, but she didn't care. One of the men offered her a mug. The cocoa tasted every bit as good as she had imagined.

Again, that eerie noise — not so frightening now that she was not alone. "Temperature's changing," Dave remarked.

"What?"

"A contraction fissure on Red's Lake," he explained. "When it gets really cold, the ice splits right across. Weird noise."

"Very," she agreed. Then someone twisted her leg, and she yelled.

"I think your ski season is over," the patrolman said. "Not a bad break, though. You'll be hiking this summer."

Jay's leg still hurt, but she laughed. A broken bone was nothing. Never in her life had she felt so lucky.

# JESSIE WEAVER

Jessie Weaver is an Olympia local and recent (ish) Evergreen graduate. She's known that she wanted to tell stories ever since her first one, a collaborative piece about a person made entirely out of bodily fluids. Her first book, published in 1997, focused on a princess who ate so much at her wedding feast that her body expanded to fill the entirety of her castle. Unfortunately, there was only ever one printing. Indeed, only one copy exists. If Jessie were at all famous, this edition, which features lavish hand drawn illustrations by the author, would surely be worth lots of money.

Jessie thanks her writing partner, Rob; her mother, Linda; and her brother Seth. Without their support this story wouldn't be possible.

# Relatively Well

Ser's favorite moment was the tug, that last feeble effort of gravity to hold her before letting go. That momentary feeling of sinking and then floating. It was something that Ser didn't talk to anyone about; a little private thing that she worried wouldn't stand up to scrutiny.

Ser had worked on spaceships for sixteen years, ever since leaving home at seventeen. She had been driven then, full of passion. She had thought that the first step would be the hardest; that once taken everything else would come to her, if not with ease, then at least without any difficulties that she couldn't overcome. Her vision had been to be both an explorer and a vagabond: a citizen of the stars. This vision would lead her sooner or later, she had been certain, to the Central Worlds. This collection of planets contained the oldest human habitations, including the original — Earth itself. They held the greatest art, the tallest buildings, and the most dazzling nightlife. And, she had been certain, the only place for a woman of her talent and determination.

As it turned out, it was easier to become a citizen of "the stars" than to gain citizenship, or even a travel visa, to the Central Worlds. Migration to those crowded planets was only intended to go in one direction: outwards. And then there was the travel time. Actually that wouldn't be so bad from her point of view. But relativity skewed things. For her it would be only months, but for the rest of the universe it would be eighteen years.

Ser had wanted to give herself time to think about it. She had been thinking about it for sixteen years and she still hadn't figured out how she felt. So she lived her life in between. She ran people and goods back and forth from colony world to colony world.

Her trade lacked the glory that she had dreamed of as a child, but there was a sort of quiet magic to it that she liked. To make your home in the vast emptiness between the stars took a certain kind of courage, she thought, a certain kind of heroism.

—

As her vessel lifted off of the surface of Korlevic, her passengers packed closely together in the windowless back, like a delicate cargo, she reflected that she was the only one seeing this beauty. The back of her ship didn't have windows because it was cheaper by far for it not to have them, and because, while she ferried people frequently, the ship was technically intended only for cargo and livestock loads. But her fares were cheap and her customers didn't usually complain. They didn't get much of chance: the accommodations were cramped enough to make anyone a little crazy on a trip of this length, so they had all been put into a drug-induced sleep.

Ser did feel a little sorry for the girl though. Before take-off, she and her co-pilot Rashad had been loading people into the cargo hold. This section of the ship was by far the largest; it dwarfed the pilots' cabins and cockpit so drastically that it reminded her of the massively bloated abdomen of a honey ant. At the moment, they were only crowding people in. The artificial gravity that allowed bunks to be installed around the outer perimeter didn't work until the ship was in orbit. Standing in the doorway, staring at the cargo hold, a small girl — was she four years old? Six? Eight? — started crying.

"I wanted to see the stars!" She had wailed plaintively. Her mother had just looked down at her with tired eyes.

"You said… You said…" the girl had cried between loud gulps of air, "you said we'd see them! You said we'd be able to see the stars! And that we'd see the planets and wave goodbye to all our friends!"

She looked up with the utter rage of a child who believes, in this moment, that her mother has committed a crime for which she can never be forgiven.

The mother, now clearly aware that her child was causing a scene, pulled her in close. She spoke a rapid train of soothing words.

"Yes, sweetie." She said, unable to quite look her furious daughter in the eyes. "I really thought we would be able to see all those things, but this is the only ship that Mommy and Daddy could afford to take us to our new home."

Ser had half-opened her mouth: imagining inviting the girl into the cockpit with her. They could experience take-off together. Ser would tell the girl to savor the moment when they first became weightless. Ser might be able to tell her that, when her ship plunged into the stars, it always made her imagine diving into a vast ocean of deep sparking waters.

She almost laughed. That possibility had felt real and surprisingly tempting for a moment. Funny: Ser normally hated kids. But reality had reasserted itself. The mother probably wouldn't want her child to be alone with a stranger, let alone some crusty space pilot. And the girl would probably just spend the whole time crying for her mother and for her friends that she had left behind. The sense of kinship that she had momentarily felt between herself and the girl dried up like a marshy winter pond that couldn't withstand the glare of summer sun.

And so, as she had done so many times before, she had taken a possibility that had seemed so bright and shimmering, for a moment, and snapped it, as if to prove to herself how brittle it had really been.

—

The day before her ship left the planet, Ser had been in the cockpit, filling out tedious paperwork for the local port authority. Rashad was in town, rounding up passengers for their next voyage. Ser had been able to fill in the blanks and check the boxes almost without looking at the pages in front of her. These forms were always the same. She had a barely interesting documentary about Earth history playing in the background, and her eyes flicked impatiently back and forth between the screen and the pages that she had propped up against the navigation console. She knew she shouldn't be writing on it, it would only mess with the screen and cause more of those annoying little white pinpricks to pop up, blending in among the stars on her navigation charts — but she couldn't be bothered to find something else to write on.

Then the screen flashed and her documentary paused. Ser frowned at it and it flashed more rapidly, emitting a soft trilling noise. A name appeared on its surface: Ilesh Joshi. Her brother. Ser considered ignoring it. She hadn't spoken to Ili for quite a while and, the longer she went without calling him, the guiltier she felt. Maybe she should call back later. Then she could have the conversation on her own terms. She could wash her hair first and put on a cleaner shirt. She would have time to remember how to rearrange her face to look happy and confident.

Sighing, she took the call.

"Hey Ser," the caller had said.

"Hey Ili."

There was a pause, in which both parties searched for words.

"You're looking good." Her brother hazarded.

Ser scowled. Her reflection shone across the surface of her brother's image on the screen and it looked anything but good.

"You never used to lie to me."

"I'm not lying to you. You do look good. You look… young."

For some reason this seemed to be the most hurtful thing that he could say. She didn't want the only thing that looked good to her brother about her life to be her relative youth. After all, it wasn't as though she was going to live any longer from her perspective. He would just die faster. And he did look older. At thirty one, he actually looked like he was in the prime of his life. He was strong and tan. And something in his eyes had changed. They were wiser, perhaps.

"Well that's relativity for you," she said, her voice both bitter and joking. He looked concerned and she hated that look of concern.

"It's been so long since we've seen each other. You haven't even come home for holidays in years. I miss you."

"I…" the rest of the words trailed off, unspoken, caught against some powerful internal barrier. And yet they seemed to echo through the hollow space of the cabin.

Ili rested his forehead briefly on the back of his fingers, revealing the rough calluses of his palms. "You know I didn't call you just so we could argue."

"Ser… Ser… Ser…" He said the name in a way that reminded her of the childhood game that they had once played: the one where you say a familiar word over and over again until you feel as though you have never heard it before.

He took a huge ragged sigh. "I actually called to tell you something."

Ser felt her chest, which had been tight with anger, sag like a deflated balloon. "Mom?" She asked in a voice that was barely louder than a whisper.

Her brother laughed, just a little. "No. It's not that. Mom's doing fine. Actually, this is good news." He smiled nervously. "I'm going to be a dad."

"Oh. Uh … uh …" Ser ran two fingers in an arc over her right eyebrow. "Congratulations."

———

That night, after the call, Ser had gone out with Rashad, as they did almost every night they were in port. There was a desolate air about this place, a boom town gone bust, and they walked through the streets in the silence that the half-empty place seemed to demand. Finally, they found a small bar that was grim, but not utterly depressing. It was still early, but a sparse handful of patrons clustered around the bar, slouching into their drinks and not looking up as Ser and Rashad walked in. The newcomers ordered their drinks and sat at a sticky little table in the corner.

Rashad Lin was a man in his late 20s, with large, heavily-lashed brown eyes and a soft face. Unlike Ser, whose family had been comfortably middle class for most of her childhood, Rashad came from one of the poorest and most crowded slums in the Central Worlds. Ser noticed that years of heavy drinking and a pilot's inactive lifestyle were finally starting to take a noticeable toll on him: he looked not just soft, but puffy, and dark blue veins were visible beneath the pale brown skin under his eyes. Right now those soft eyes already had the slightly unfocused quality which showed he'd started early. He'd been starting earlier and earlier lately. He'd passed a half empty flask on the way to the bar, and Ser was almost certain that he'd filled it fresh that morning while she made her coffee.

"So. I got a call today."

"Oh yeah?" Rashad replied, a little bored. "From your fam? They're still calling you? You'd think they'd have given up by now."

"Yeah. From my brother."

Ser frowned and twirled the tiny straws around in her drink, sending the ice cubes clanking.

"And how's he doing? Still cataloging plants?"

"Yeah, probably."

Ser took a slow sip at her drink. It was a bitter acid thinly coated in sweetness.

"Rashad?"

"Yeah?" He asked, his eyes staring off at a screen that was flashing incongruously cheerful images in the other corner of the bar.

"Do you ever miss your sister?"

"My sister?" He asked distractedly. "Which one?"

Ser had forgotten that he had more than one. She thought of herself as pretty close to Rashad, but she didn't know that much about his youth. He just didn't really talk about it most of the time, though what he did say fascinated her.

Seeing her confused look, Rashad explained that his older sister had been shipped out to a prison colony when he was a small child.

"Oh, right. Well, the younger one then."

"I mean, yeah. Of course I do. Sometimes."

"Do think you would, you know, visit her if you could? If somehow the whole relativity thing wasn't a problem and you could just be there?"

Rashad's eyes had already drifted back to the screen.

"I mean, I dunno man, maybe. Probably not. Not at this point. I mean, she was always kind of boring, and now it's been, what, twenty years plus the eight or nine I've been out here. Naw. What would we talk about?"

Rashad turned back to Ser.

"But why are we talking about that shit? Come on; let's find another place to drink. This place is dead."

—

The voyage was much like any other: long, with moments of beauty and wonder floating in a sea of boredom. Ser still hadn't made a decision and she felt no closer to doing so. Maybe the news really didn't affect anything.

Sometimes she felt like a ship whose engines had failed and which would continue just drifting along its current course, forever. Sometimes she lay on her little cot, staring at the riveted walls that curled around her like ribs, and felt trapped. She felt as though she could not get up. She could not face the false promises of infinity offered by the stars or the limitations offered by her ship, her body, her life, and her destiny. She couldn't stand the idea of going up to the cockpit and looking out and seeing that she was not special, that she was little bigger or more important than one of the flecks of dust that floated through her field of vision, illuminated for a moment as it passed under a light and then flashing back into invisibility.

There were limits to how much the ship actually needed a human touch; she knew that really she and Rashad were just nannies to the sophisticated computer system which actually did most of the piloting. But, once she finally dragged her body out of bed and into the cockpit, she did watch the stars. Her week in the planet's polluted metropolis, with its too bright sunlight and grim orange night sky, had served to somewhat revive her love for the stars.

About a week into the trip, Ser's ship came into close visual range of the system's only gas giant. It was a massive and beautiful thing to stare at while she sat in her long-johns, her feet resting on the console and a tepid cup of last shift's coffee in her hand. She could have moved her feet and sat up properly in the chair, using the console for its intended purpose. She could have retrieved the planet's name and a whole list of numbers, too big for the human brain to really comprehend, in seconds. She could have compared those figures to those of the gas giants from her own system, or to the First System's Jupiter, a world that had been named after a god and not just some scientist or explorer. But she didn't. It was too early in her shift for numbers and there was no point in comparing one mystifying wonder to another.

The planet swirled with dust and gasses: brown and gold and red and even purple. She wished that the little girl could see this. She wished that her brother could see this.

Ser wished that she had been able to convince Ili to leave home with her. The fantasy had been acted out so many times as children that she had almost seen it as a foregone conclusion. Out in the forest behind their family's house, the two had played space pilots and interplanetary explorers. Ili's favorite game had always been Pioneers, bravely exploring unmapped planets and then colonizing them (which, in the game, usually consisted of building a fort out of sticks and then creating make-believe, foresty versions of ordinary things). But Ser would always choose the game, meting out the roles to be played, and Ili had always played along. She supposed that she should have noticed eventually that he was more interested in mushrooms and mosses than he was in stars and planets. She supposed that it shouldn't have been a shock when he told her that he wanted to stay and study to become a botanist.

Ser watched the gas giant for a long time. She was acutely aware of how tiny and fragile her ship was next to it. Of how just one of those vast, swirling storms could swallow up, not just this ship and all its passengers, but the entire world from which they had come. There was both a terror and a peace to it, she thought. It was something like the awe that she had felt when she had first seen the ocean when she was seven or eight. There had been a great roaring whisper that had pushed every other sound from her ears. Swells had danced in and out, mesmerizing her. A particularly strong one had rushed greedily up covering her legs in water to the knees so quickly it had made her gasp. As the wave pulled away she had felt it dragging at her, making her stumble. She had thought that the ocean would take her: that she would be subsumed and utterly obliterated in its fathomless might.

But Ser felt something else as she looked out the windows. Boredom. Of course, at first such an emotion would be unimaginable, but slowly it had snuck in. She wondered if it would ever be possible to stop loving the stars, if seeing something often enough could rob it entirely of its power to move, to awe. Well, that hadn't happened yet anyway. But she wondered. Was she drying up inside? Turning into something brittle and hollow, empty and incapable of feeling?

Sometimes while she sat in the cockpit she thought about calling her brother, just to listen to him talk. Other times she flicked randomly through information about the Central Worlds: tourist guides, visa materials, job postings. But she never made more than listless half-motions in either direction.

—

As her ship neared its destination Ser went to the hold to help the passengers prepare for landing. She had been checking on these people every other shift or so while they had slept their drug-induced sleep. She hadn't been able to stop herself from walking by the little girl every time. Why was it, she had wondered, that perfectly ordinary children like this one become beautiful when they sleep?

Now the drugs were beginning to wear off and, in all of the tall narrow bunks that filled the hold, people were stirring. This was one of

Ser's favorite times on any journey in which they took on passengers. They were funny to watch with their comically slack mouths and wide eyes as they stared uncomprehending across the hold. They would crane their necks up, only to find themselves staring down, looking across the rotating hold at the tops of the bunks on the other side and their occupants.

Ser spotted the girl's family almost immediately. They were across the hold diagonally from her. The children seemed to be shaking off the drugs more rapidly than the adults; they had all clambered up to the top bunk and were now laughing, pointing, and covering their eyes theatrically with their hands only to peak out from them again. The girl was clinging to the hand of a child a couple of years younger than her and pointing out across the gap at a child on a bunk near Ser. She heard a peal of high pitched laughter from above her head. A powerful pang of nostalgia swam through her body and for a moment she just stood, watching the clambering children. As she did, layers of complexity and disquiet were peeled back from the universe. Ser smiled, allowing enough optimism to creep through the crack in her guard to let herself be momentarily swept up in the joy of the children..

—

Their destination was a large, dry red planet — good for mining and not much else. Even from space it was ugly. Wonky rectangles of gigantic strip mining operations were etched into its surface like someone's poor idea of abstract art.

Rashad was at the controls as they descended. They passed the upper atmosphere ports where the larger vessels were docked. Here grim transport freighters waited to serve their singular purpose: carting away the earth of this planet. They dwarfed her vessel as drastically as humans do an insect. Row after row of gargantuan rectangular boxes jutted from the freighters' central axles. Ser frowned and looked away.

—

The port town was large and industrial. Countless identical warehouses, all made from the same reddish concrete, ran out in neat rows from the port. But it wasn't hard to find a bar despite this. There was one very near the dock, identical to all the other buildings, but decked out with large round lights in blue and red and green. A large crowd of miners and dock workers in dirty overalls were milling outside, gossiping and laughing raucously.

The inside of the bar was filled with similar sorts. Voices from all around her yelled to be heard over the music and each other. Ser and Rashad steered around them.

It was Rashad who noticed the small group of pilots who had blockaded themselves into a table in the far corner, their backs turned against the possibility of being joined by locals. Rashad tapped one of them lightly, and Ser could see his shoulder muscles constrict beneath his shirt. A couple of pilots laughed, recognizing Ser and Rashad, and when he turned around the guy smiled apologetically and offered his hand.

"Hey!" He exclaimed. "Come join our table you two!"

The man was short and ruddy-faced with a pug-like nose that looked as though it had been broken at some point. Ser and Rashad had run into him a couple of times, but Ser couldn't remember his name, and it was clear that he couldn't remember theirs either. This was normal among pilots, who rarely saw each other often enough to remember names from one time to the next.

Rashad said, "Hey," in return and affably clapped the man on the back.

"I'm Rashad and this is Ser," he said, turning to the table.

It didn't take long for them to be deep into pilot's chatter and for Ser to be deep into her third or fourth drink. It was at roughly this point that someone mentioned the freighters. The pilots talked about them in disgust; these were all independents that ran small scale operations. They naturally scorned those who did corporate work.

"And a couple of them are headed for the Central Worlds," a short woman, whose untrimmed hair flopped shaggily around her face, pointed out. "Can you imagine that? The voyage itself doesn't take too long, but when you get back you've lost forty years . I mean, you step onto one of those things, and when you get off a few months later you're twenty years into the future."

"Actually, I think it's more like 18 or so," Ser responded.

"Oh? You been thinking about it a lot have you?"

"Ser wants to go to the Central Worlds." Rashad said. "I keep telling her that there's nothing too exiting about skyscrapers or those old buildings, but she can't let it go."

The table laughed. Ser bit her lip and glared at Rashad.

"So what?" The short woman demanded. "You're going to whore yourself out to a freighter so you can do it?"

"Maybe." Ser replied defensively. "I mean, it's not that big of a deal."

"Oh, you don't think so? Well I know what you should do," The red-faced man said. "I think the pilot for one of those ships is in here. Petra Petropoulos. She's a real interesting lady. I think you two'd get along real well. Who knows, maybe she'll even offer you a job."

Clearly he was trying to call her bluff. Ser hated being put on the spot, but she wasn't going to give him the benefit of seeing her back out.

"Fine," she said.

"All right, fine." The man said, laughing. "Let's go."

The red-faced pilot rose to his feet, a bit unsteady, and made a sweeping gesture at Ser to follow. She did, and the rest of the table followed them. They crossed the bar to a stairway against a side wall which led up to a smaller, less crowded, upper floor. There was a long string of small rectangular windows with a concrete bar jutting out from underneath them. A woman was sitting in the corner, nursing a tall glass and staring out the window.

"Petra," the man addressed her. For a moment it seemed as though she hadn't heard, but then slowly she swiveled her stool around to look at them. There was something strange about the woman, but it was hard to place exactly what. Her clothes certainly were a little odd, she wore a high collared shirt of a kind that Ser was not familiar with. Also, she noticed that the woman had a tattoo, it appeared to be of a snake, and she saw its muscular body winding confidently up the side of the woman's neck. It slid behind her ear and disappeared into her graying hair, which was pulled back into a simple pony tail. The snake reappeared on the other side of her head, its mouth poised by her ear, as if to whisper secrets into it. Ser thought that she remembered hearing that head tattoos like this had been popular among early settlers, though she couldn't remember why. She was fairly certain that for full effect, the hair should have been shaved, at least where the tattoo was, so that it would be fully visible.

"What...?"

"Well, this lovely young woman expressed an interest in sailing on your ship. She's a very, very talented pilot, and I thought that you'd enjoy talking to her."

The woman looked at Ser, her eyes suddenly sharp and unblinking, locking Ser into her gaze.

"Oh? Is that so? You ever work on a freighter?"

"No, ma'am."

Ser wondered why she had called her "ma'am;" it wasn't like her to use empty niceties. Something about this woman intimidated her.

"But you work as a pilot? So you're one of the independents then, jumping back and forth on short trips. You've never been in for the long haul."

"I think I could do it, ma'am." Ser straightened her spine and pulled her shoulders back. She didn't like what this woman was implying.

"Well, sit down." Petra was suddenly welcoming, making a sweeping gesture at the little stool beside hers. Ser hesitated and sat down. Petra turned on her companions.

"The rest of you can go now," she said brusquely. "I promise that I'll return your friend to you just as I found her."

"Yes, ma'am!" The red-faced man replied with an exaggerated salute. The group of pilots turned and stumbled, laughing, down the stairs. Rashad was the last to turn; he shot her a concerned little grin. "You gonna be OK?"

"I'm fine, thanks. I'll be back down soon."

The others now gone, Petra turned to Ser and smiled the smile of someone sharing an inside joke.

"All right. Now we're alone. Tell me why you want to sail on a freighter. You indies don't usually like corporate work."

"Well it would be a great opportunity..."

"Bullshit. You know as well as I do that those words don't mean anything. An opportunity for what? You have your own operation; you don't exactly need to further your career. Is it the pay? That's certainly attractive; you'd get four or five times as much as you would working your own operation for a comparable period. But I don't think that's it."

She locked Ser into her vise tight gaze again.

"No. You want something else. I recognize it. You want to explore.

You want to see."

"Yes!"

"Mmm-hmm. And it is a wonderful thing. Exploration..."

She stared out the window, her vision trailing across the long line of rectangular buildings and off to sharp red cliffs that cut across the horizon like a serrated knife. Petra turned to Ser, her face suddenly bright.

"Will you walk with me pilot?"

"Umm... but my friends..."

"Will be just fine until you get back." Petra replied firmly.

Ser drew in her breath and then expelled it in a slow sigh. "OK. All right. I guess. Why not?" She stood and pulled on her black faux-leather jacket. "Let's go."

The floor downstairs was even more crowded than before. After pushing through the mass of sweating bodies, Ser welcomed the wave of cool air that rolled over her body as she opened the door with a relieved sigh.

Petra, who proved to be quite tall and lanky on her feet, set a fast pace, pushing off along the brightly lit street towards the great darkness that seemed to hang at the end of it. Ser glanced up and saw a handful of brave stars that had bullied their way past the street lights to shine faintly down at her. She and Petra walked down the street, past cold, empty warehouses, for perhaps five minutes before Ser nervously tried to resume conversation with her suddenly very driven companion.

"So it sounds like you've done a lot of traveling?" she asked weakly.

"Shhh! We can talk when we get there."

"Get where?"

Petra's thin shoulders shrugged. "Wherever we're going."

The warehouses were beginning to thin out, and it wasn't long before they were walking between large complexes which each occupied several blocks. But eventually, even these gave way to the night, and they were walking along a bare road, brilliant under the white orbs that lit it and surrounded by utter blackness. Suddenly Petra turned, striding purposefully off of the road and into the darkness. By this point Ser was a little bit frightened. Petra seemed like she might be a little crazy. Ser was OK with that, but what if she was a dangerous kind of crazy?

She followed Petra into the darkness. And soon the darkness was not even darkness. The further they got from the road the more the stars asserted themselves and her vision adapted to the night. They were walking along a thin path in a sparse and rocky desert plateau. Hearty little plants poked here and there through the ground, and the red earth stretched out far ahead of her, glimmering mystically in the starlight. Finally Petra stopped. A wide flat rock sat welcomingly just to the side of the trail.

"Sit with me?"

"Sure."

They sat on the rock and looked ahead at the glowing expanse of earth and sky. For a long minute they were silent.

Petra sighed and leaned back on her long arms, kicking her legs out ahead of her.

"People call Sekhar a barren world, but I could never call such beauty barren."

Ser nodded. She had been here several times but never stepped out of the spaceport.

"It will be different the next time I'm here of course. Thirty-six years. This spot may not even be here."

Ser nodded again, and then thinking that this might not be enough said, "Yeah."

When Petra didn't say anything else, Ser realized that perhaps it fell on her to continue the conversation. "How many times have you been here?"

"Here? You mean this world? I'm not sure." She closed her eyes and seemed to be counting in her head. "Five? Six?"

"And each time were you voyaging from the Central Worlds?" Ser asked, unable to keep the wonder from her voice.

Petra nodded, her eyes sad and distant.

"How did you get started, you know, doing what you do?"

"To explain that, I'd have to explain a lot of other things that you colonists have probably forgotten by now. Hell, I've probably forgotten a lot of it, though it wasn't all that long ago for me. At that time, to be one of the pioneers was considered a brave and noble undertaking, perhaps the best thing that an otherwise average person like me could do for my people. A very patriotic decision, but then I wasn't really the most patriotic of folk."

"So why then?"

"I guess I was like you. I felt trapped. I wanted to explore. My ego played its part, too; I wanted to be one of the first to step onto new worlds, to see uncharted lands with my own eyes."

Ser mulled this over in silence. Petra was a pioneer, one of the Pioneers, the first to come to the outer worlds.

"So I got on one of the ships, one of the long arcs. Back then, the journey wasn't so quick as it is now. When I woke up from stasis, I was in a new world."

"I really don't think that you can understand what that was like. I wonder if I'm the only one alive who still remembers. Well, that's the way of things, I suppose. Time moves forward and we forget."

"Except for space itself, I had never seen something so vast as the plateaus of this world. Such openness after the constant press of the cities, the narrow living spaces and narrower lives… I suppose I fell in love. But love so often fades, and I found myself missing the crowds that I had once chafed against, the faces that I had lost.

"A word formed in my mind and began to take on a magical quality: 'Home.' It came to me when I woke up on this strange world and when I went to sleep. I thought it with every movement of my tired muscles as I worked to build this place.

"The word was just a mantra, meaningless I told myself, because I would never get a chance to go home. Home was gone. I knew that I'd never see it again, and if I did it would be so changed that I'd barely recognize it. But then, I got a chance to return. A crewmember on one of the few ships going back, filled to the brim with mineral samples, died unexpectedly. They needed someone who could do his work, and I could. I wasn't the only one who wanted to go back , but I was the one who got to.

"The whole trip back, or at least the parts I was awake for, that mantra kept going: 'Home, home, home'…

"But when I got back, I shouldn't have been surprised, but I was: everything had changed. There was hardly a building or living person left which I could recognize as having known. My family had seen me as a hero; there was a little shrine with my picture in my nephew's house. But he didn't know me; and though he and everyone who was left celebrated my return with a party, they were clearly disappointed that I had betrayed my heroic reputation by giving up and returning home. My mother was gone, which I had expected. But I had hoped to see my sister again …

"When I realized that there was little left on my former planet for me, I set off on a journey. I traveled until I ran out of money, jumping from world to world looking at art and buildings, and mountains and trees. And then, broke, and with no skills suitable for civilized life on those worlds, I took to space again. I signed on with a freighter and since then I have been jumping back and forth, back and forth.

"I still travel sometimes. I get more money than I know what to do with, and I have been able to see almost everything that is called a 'marvel' on the Central and Outer worlds, and many other things besides, some not so marvelous."

"Do you ever regret it?"

"Of course. Sometimes. But I would have regretted staying, too." She turned to Ser. "We all make choices. And every opportunity taken is a hundred missed. But that's life. I can't be too ungrateful. I have been very lucky in a lot of ways."

There was silence for a while. Ser felt words building up in her, but it took a bit of effort to actually get them past her lips.

"My little brother is going to have a baby."

"And does that change anything for you?"

"Yes. Well, not really. I guess I don't know. It makes the decision harder I guess."

"And that's what it boils down to for you right now, isn't it? You have to make a decision."

"Yes," Ser said, then a little desperately. "What do you recommend?"

Petra laughed. "Me? I'd recommend that you go. But then, I need a good hand." Her smile slowly faded and she became serious again. "But then, you don't really need me to tell you what to do, any more than you need me to tell you that I can't tell you what to do. So now I'll ask you: what are you going to do?"

Ser stared out into the night. One of the planet's moons had come out and hung like a giant silver coin. She imagined that she had attached her choices to it and tossed it up into the air. Which side did she hope would land face up? The moon hung, shimmering with possibility.

A smile slowly appeared on her face. She knew what she wanted. She reached up into the sky and closed her hand around the moon, clutching briefly onto all of her options. Her hand lowered and the moon shone in the sky as brightly as ever.

—

The straight trunks of the tall, white false ginkgos surrounding the path gleamed white in the bright sun. High above, clumps of their little fan-shaped leaves glowed a brilliant green with captured sunlight. All around her stood some kind of tall fern-like plants that grew out of the ground in a singular frond almost as tall as she was, their tips still curled into tight fists. Their slightly translucent flesh seemed to pulse with the insatiable fierceness of new spring life.

The path was curling slowly downward and Ser was slowly falling behind. She didn't mind. She concentrated step by step on the placement of her feet, and on balancing the weight that kept rolling and shifting on her shoulders. The muscles in her legs pulled against the tilt of the hill, keeping her upright.

Ili and Anika were waiting for her at the end of the hill. A little stream cut through the tiny valley, trees leaning delicately over like fancy ladies daintily testing the water.

"Aun' Ser! Aun' Ser!" A small piping voice called out from above her head. Tiny hiking boots jiggled excitedly in her hands.

Ser walked over to her brother and let him gently lift the small child from her shoulders and place her on the ground. The girl ran to the water and immediately began kicking up gigantic splashes of water which shimmered briefly in the air before falling back down into the rippling surface.

## Barbara Yunker

Born and raised in Anchorage, Alaska, Barbara is a graduate of the University of Washington and The Evergreen State College. Her stories have appeared in *Slightly West* and *On Uneven Ground*. She is the author of *Teachings of the Sea and Distant Shores*, a collection of poetry and essays inspired by three around-the-world voyages as a participant in the University of Virginia Semester at Sea program.

With her husband Dick, she has bicycled across the United States, walked across England, walked the Pacific Crest Trail in Washington, the John Muir Trail in California, The Camino de Santiago in Spain, and The Walker's Haute Route through the Alps from Chamonix to Zermatt. They have climbed Mt. Adams, Mt. Whitney, Mt. Kilimanjaro, and Mt. Fuji. Barbara has independently climbed Mt. Rainier and the holy mountain of Sri Pada in Sri Lanka.

The Yunkers own and manage Puget View, a bed and breakfast turned vacation rental, and live in an historic log home on Puget Sound with their fat cat named Señor.

# The Fire Finder

Forty feet below, Rocky Mountain elk browse on frosty low-bush huckleberry. Across the snowy, eastern flank of Mount Hood, dawn spreads itself — like a huge comforter the color of robins' eggs.

"Get up," Dick coaxes, rousing me from the single bunk in which we have slept head to toe. "You have to see the beauty-ness." In a fire lookout ten miles east of Mount Hood in the national forest of north central Oregon, my husband and I — alone — celebrate our twenty-second wedding anniversary.

The idea for our getaway came when our oldest daughter gifted her dad with a book for Father's Day: *How to Rent a Fire Lookout in the Pacific Northwest.* "Just in case," she said, "there is someplace in these parts you don't know about. Thank you, Dad, for sharing so much of the northwest with me all my life."

Much of the northwest woods was Dick. In him there seemed to be some human-wilderness symbiosis, developed cell by cell, summer after summer, as he hiked and backpacked miles of rugged Oregon backcountry as a teenager. One of these summers, or two, Dick worked fire crew — stories the kids and I loved to hear — of high school boys running around in underpants and hard hats, one the "head hoe" another the "ass hoe" of the group. We snickered, but Dick always corrected, "That was a job description, not an insult." But by the time Dick graduated from high school, he'd logged so many hours in the woods it was easy to believe he'd been raised not so much in the natural world as by it. Wilderness — yes, parents too — but wilderness had imprinted itself on Dick as he changed from child to man.

⁓

This morning, Mt. Hood is all over our western exposure — a huge linen napkin folded in a perky triangle. "Hey," I say. "Wasn't it around here we went cross-country skiing when Brittany was a baby?"

"Mount Hood meadows," Dick says pointing dead ahead. That day, with her in the backpack, we wrapped her mittened but cold hands in another layer of all we had — a spare pair of Dick's wool socks, so large they came up to her armpits.

In college, the selection of Dick's major had been no question. Foresters, after all, got paid to be in the woods. And it was funny how Dick's understanding of the natural world surfaced, as predictably, it seemed, as a whale spouts to breathe. Often on the most casual of outings — "That's pseudotsuga. See how the bracts on the cones are three-pointed?" Or geology. "Look at that formation, how it's uplifted." Followed by an impromptu dissertation from *The Roadside Geology of Oregon* or Washington. The land, and the life that it supported, defined who Dick was.

And he brought this to our relationship. On our first date, mushroom hunting. "Want to go? The chantrelles are out."

—

Naked, we sit on wooden folding chairs, eating breakfast of instant grits, coffee, granola bars, saying little. Brilliant morning sunlight jolts through row upon row of the small-paned, wood-cased windows on each side of the fifty year-old lookout. It's comfortable and warm on my bare skin.

Silently I fall into mulling over how long we'd been together. How we survived — just barely — the disillusionment phase of our marriage and how, because of it, we became stronger, gentler, and wise enough — when given the choice between isolation and enrichment — we embraced the latter. How close I'd come to leaving, and how stupid it all seemed. So intoxicating to be flattered by a bachelor high school classmate at my twentieth high school reunion. How exotic his trip to Egypt. How worldly and wonderful. How I wanted it, and him, and my life to be worldly, and wonderful, and exotic too. Blind-sided by something that would have ruined everything.

Or on the beach in Santa Barbara — where I thought I'd find my perfect life — and almost didn't come home — until the voice of reason spoke loud enough to drown out all of love's disappointments — the $4,000 Dick lifted from our savings without telling me. "But Barbara," the voice said, "where are the people that you love, and that love you?"

I smooth and twist the empty wrapper of my granola bar. To the north, forty miles away, hovers the snowy, flat-top of Mt. St. Helens. How Cathy cried when that blew, pulverizing her summer camp on Spirit Lake. We picnicked there before the eruption — on a part of the mountain that is no longer.

The date of the eruption is easy to remember. A week to the day after our wedding, in the front yard of our home on Puget Sound. The one we still live in. All these years we've stayed, never dreaming it would be so long. In our log house, with mountains across the bay. Motifs from my childhood in Alaska.

Easily, my thoughts warp through time. And I'm in the living room of my childhood home where the Chugach Range spills in, wallpapering my childhood. Wilderness was there — as close as Mt. Hood today.

You'd think, growing up in a place like Alaska, you'd never want to leave, but by the time I graduated from high school — I didn't understand it then, but do now — I related to the outdoors the way you can — if you're not careful — relate to the person you've been married to for twenty-two years: with a lack of appreciation.

But I wanted out. In the Alaskan vernacular I wanted to "go Outside" which means — and I most sorely did — I wanted to go outside of Alaska.

Now, that all sounds crazy, but then, spending a freshman year of college in Southern California and a semester traveling around the world seemed — well — what I thought I needed

But as the number of my post-high school years increased — and without really being conscious of it — my life became increasingly urban. I ditched winter sports. Too much of a sissy — I guess — to put on my own tire chains. Enrolled at the UW in metro Seattle. I suppose I was too focused — too stupid — or maybe nothing more than just too darn lazy — to get out of town.

At all.

After college I opted for a fancy marketing position, with a sales quota, a house, and — for the longest time I couldn't figure it out — a haunting emptiness. Depression. I'd ask myself, "What's wrong with you?" And all I could articulate was that I needed a change.

To make myself feel better I sold the house, quit the job, terminated my committed relationship with a Datsun 1600 roadster — and took off. Another three month trip around the world to work on my life as jigsaw puzzle. Hoping to get the puzzle box open, the pieces out on the table right side up, work the edges, and then the middle, until I could figure out what the blasted piece was that was missing and where it could possibly have gotten lost.

I summered in a twelve by fourteen foot cabin. A shed really — on Puget Sound. With no hot water. Bathing was a series of splashes, while I stood on a heavy-duty trash bag with the sides rolled down to form a little dike. My indoor plumbing consisted of a toilet that did not back up — well, not usually — so long as you adhered to the house rule: yellow, let it mellow; brown flush it down. But it stunk.

My roommates were an army of mice.

I wrote poetry, essays. I wore torn up army pants and didn't shave my legs. All this, I believed, would somehow bring me closer to the epiphany I sought, which, toward the end of August, I guess it did. What I needed — and this revealed itself with the strongest sense of knowing. What I needed — was a hit of wilderness.

—

Aside from the bunk and the little table and chairs, one solar-powered light, and a wood stove is all that furnishes the lookout, except for a wooden pedestal about four feet high, exactly at the center of the room, lined with crude shelves on each of its four sides — storage for food, books, dishes.

And on top of the pedestal — "What is it?" I ask Dick.

"It's a fire finder," he says, pressing his finger in the center of the map that covers the top of the pedestal. In the center of the map I see the concentric topographic markings that delineate exactly where we are — Five Mile Butte — us. "We're here," says Dick. "This is the cabin. When there's a forest fire, the person manning the lookout takes a compass bearing on the fire and estimates the distance. In another lookout they'll do the same. The intersection of their bearings pinpoint the fire."

—

Still naked, I brush my teeth at the old-fashioned wall-hung sink in the
northwest corner of the cabin. Straight ahead, pops the snowy cone
of Mt. Adams. My thoughts follow the east ridge, the treeless, pumice
strewn moonscape, to the climber's bivouac called Lunch Counter
where Dick and I camped many years ago, as the staging area for our
summit climb — my first summit of any of the Cascade volcanoes.
"Plan B" after a botched Rainier summit attempt the day before.

And there, just this side of Adams — that's it: Indian Heaven
Wilderness! Where we camped with Dick's folks many Septembers,
berry picking for mountain huckleberries. Like bees among honey,
fingers undulate like the legs of little centipedes through the crimson
bushes. Miniscule blue-purple fruit plunk-plunks into our coffee can
buckets. Hands, lips, teeth the color of hydrangeas from so much
snitching and tasting.

—

I spit into the sink and think how silly. The drain ends just beyond the
floor boards. Spit, blowing in the wind.

Next to Adams and behind I can see Rainier. From its eastern flank,
Mt. Tahoma juts out. Just like the horn of a rhinoceros.

I imagine the crevasses of the huge Emmons glacier — largest
glacier in the States outside of Alaska — stretching, twisting from
Camp Sherman to the base of Tahoma, not far from the Sunrise visitor
center at Rainier where I took Brittany, as a three-year-old, on her
first alpine hike. In my mind she is as she is in the photo from that day,
hair in bunched up pigtails, arms stretched high and full of joy — as
if to grasp something enormous, something wonderful. The day she
believed she could touch a glacier. "I'm touching it mommy. I'm
touching the glacier." Who was I to say?

I blink. And Tahoma is below me, an island of rock, punching
through an ocean of clouds, and I am at the top of Disappointment
Cleaver, the day of my successful Rainier summit. The day that was
a gift — of fair weather and a blessed guide who pulled me over the
summit crater rim.

Inside the summit crater I sit in sunshine, lunching on a ham
sandwich at fourteen thousand feet.

And I think of Bill.

Our ninety year-old neighbor who worked decades as a Mt. Rainier climbing ranger, after whom the ranger hut, Butler Shelter, at the Muir climbing camp, is named.

Then — Bill is with me again — as he was in visions during the days just before the climb. For good luck, I wear a badge of Bill's, safety-pinned to a shoe lace necklace.

The badge is small, round, royal blue with a white cross. The word "rescue" in caps across the top. "Thank you," I say as if Bill were there to hear me. In his Smokey the Bear ranger suit and hat, Bill is ahead of me on a snowfield. He turns, and in his folksy Tennessee drawl — so gentle and encouraging — I hear him say, "Awl he'p ya. Awl he'p ya." It was Bill's energy, wasn't it, on the crater rim?

And then the day after the climb, at sea level, at church — how I cried uncontrollably. About Bill. About the climb. About how much the so-called success of it all seemed to have so little to do with me and so much to do with something else — beyond me. The godsend of good weather, no accidents, no problems. Grace given, grace received.

From the look-out, the trails Dick and I have hiked scroll before me like clips from an old movie. Summerland, Burroughs Mountain, Mystic Lake. The magnificent moraines of the Carbon Glacier, the calendar page reflection of Mirror Lake. Avalanche lilies, paint brush at Indian Henry's Hunting Ground. Yes, I say to myself, there is still snow there. And I feel again — with an ache — the uneasy, exciting undulation of the bridge, that spooky suspension bridge a hundred feet above the deafening glacial torrent of Tahoma Creek.

And there — just east of Rainier, like white caps suspended above the horizon, float the pinnacles of the Goat Rocks Wilderness, high points along Washington's Pacific Crest Trail. We'd hiked it all. Where Dick backpacked several days alone when he needed to sort things out after his divorce. Where I went when I needed to prove to myself I could pitch my own damn tent and not freak out on an overnight alone.

Where Dick took Cathy and her brother Steve, to the top of Old Snowy in the early '70's before I knew them. The kids so much older now than their Dad was then. Them, too, I see in the photo of that day. Steve signs the register, grinning. The register he will sign again when he returns as a teen on a multi-day, no-parents-allowed, trek.

The same Goat Rocks where decades later, an angel will guide Dick and Brittany and me safely down from the witchy south buttress of Gilbert Peak. The elegant, sexy ridge on the cover of the National Geographic coffee table book *America's Most Magnificent Mountains* — on our coffee table back home.

Gilbert, I mutter to myself. Where we shimmy around boulders the size of SUV's, and look anywhere but down the 2,000 foot drop-off on either side of the ridge. "I'm not going back down this Devil's Highway," I announce. To which our angel — who had to fly there because we hadn't seen another soul in two days — responds, seated calmly on a ledge a few hundred feet above us. "I wouldn't either," he shouts, "scares the B-Jesus out of me." Angel Phil follows us to the summit. "But how the hell are we getting down?" To which Phil explains, "I came up the glacier this morning. It'll be softer now. I think you can make it. Just step exactly where I step. You'll be fine."

Then, we are down. "I will leave you here," Phil says. "I am going out another way." And he is gone.

—

I squirt a swish of water from my water bottle into my mouth, rinse, spit, tap my toothbrush on the edge of the sink.

In another Goat Rocks flash, Dick leads a YMCA group above timberline along a snow-scuffed ridge. I chuckle. He is wearing that old white shirt. The frayed button-down he loved for hiking because it was cool and the long sleeves kept the bugs off. That shirt, yellowed now and rust-stained from too many years on a wire hanger, hangs, even yet, in Dick's closet — one of many things he'll never use again, but could never bring himself to throw away. Because the shirt — like the gift from Cathy that brought us here — was also a Father's Day gift — from Brittany. The words "My Daddy" on the front in the hand-painted lettering of a nine year-old. On the back, embellished with Jackson Pollock splotches of hot pink paint, "Dedicated to My Dad on the Father's Day of 1992."

"Hey," I say, zipping my toothbrush and toothpaste into a sandwich-sized Ziploc, "look at the Olympics."

In the distance, beyond the Cascades, I make out a white, low, bric-a-brac line, the 7,000 foot peaks that pounce from the far shore of the saltwater bay of Puget Sound — our front yard. The mountains where wild goats ate apples from our hands.

From the living room, dining room, kitchen of the home we've lived in for over two decades, these peaks — like the Chugach Range of my childhood — have been the back drop of our lives. As much in our home, a part of our lives as draperies and furniture. Stunning in their youthful pinkness of fresh snow cover. Stirring in us a sense of rightness and strength when we have beheld them as the blue-black monoliths behind which the July sun sets, toasting the sky a psychedelic gold and red and blue. These mountains are the neighbors we have invited in, the silent witnesses of our strange, small lives, which — because of their presence — we are better off and enriched.

In the warmth of the moment I ponder equally warm, summer afternoons when I sit on the front steps of my home, a cool drink in hand, and read these peaks left to right, reciting their names — Ellinor, Washington, Constance, Walker — as though they are my children.

"And that," says Dick, pointing to the southeast, "is where Dad and I used to go deer hunting." Beyond the vast ridges of the high desert of central and eastern Oregon, the Antelope Valley and the John Day Fossil Beds. There, too, are relics of family vacations. Last good memories with grandparents now dead.

Slowly I turn to each compass point of my surroundings. The hills, the valleys, the peaks acknowledge me as though we are cousins who played together as children and now see one another again for the first time in a long time.

This land, I realize, has been our playground. The neighborhood of our true growing up, the proving ground of our marriage wherein resides a mute sense of common history, one needing the other to validate that what has been shared is true. Our lives are embedded here. In this landscape our experience is laid down, fossilized, imprinted, indelible. We know this land. We are as intimate with it as we are with one another. High Hut, High Rock, Old Snowy, Gilbert Peak — the landforms embrace me, presenting themselves as pages from the album of our life together.

Each one a totem, a cairn, a waypoint — as fixed in us, as fixed in the land, as is the fire finder at the center of the room in which I stand naked and warm.

Kim K. O'Hara is a high school math
and publications teacher who lives in
Lacey, WA, and relishes frequent visits
from two irresistible granddaughters.
She loves reading, writing, and
recreational math, but seldom gets in
the mood for housework. You can reach
her by email at kimkohara.author@
gmail.com. Sign up for new book
notifications at pagesandnumbers.com.

# The Strandweaver

*The teacher tapped his pencil. TAP TAP tap-tap-tap TAP. Precise. His eyes narrowed as he watched the five-year-olds work on their designs.*
*The twelfth time through the pattern, he varied it, a hundredth of a second delay on the last TAP. Audrey flinched. The teacher smiled.*

—

The next day, a new teacher came to get Audrey and take her to a new classroom. "I haven't finished my design," she said.

"We're giving you different designs," her new teacher told her. "Much nicer, see?"

But Audrey didn't like the new designs. They were arranged all wrong. They wouldn't lie flat on the paper. She tried to press them down with her hand, but the lines dodged her and slipped through her fingers. They hummed out of tune. She scowled.

The teacher laid some tools by her elbow. Her hand found what she needed, and she poked at the bad lines until they wove around and through each other. The colors blended. The hum was right.

The new teacher took away the paper and gave her a bigger one. More complicated.

—

*Audrey's father was reluctant. Audrey needed time to be a kid, he said.*
*Her mother prevailed. "Let her make a difference. She has a talent."*
*In the end, it had never been their choice. The Special Talents Entry Program took whomever it wanted. Talking with the parents was just a formality.*

—

It had been a year, and Audrey was very fast at fixing bad lines now. Her designs were no longer flat, but came packed up in big shapes. Most of the time, she didn't even need to use the tools.
She could whisper to the strands—not out loud, but in her mind— and coax them into place. She used her fingers to show them where they belonged.

She had learned that she wasn't just supposed to make them sound right and look right. The teachers said they were machines, and they needed to work right too. They gave the shapes a name: "artifacts." Audrey liked that name, because it sounded like painting and drawing.

—

*The teachers conferred. She was beyond anything they'd encountered before. She repaired artifacts in minutes, restoring them to full functionality.*

*Some were useless, of course, because they were made for beings with different sensory organs and body shapes. Others had functions they could only guess at.*

*Except for the most rudimentary, her methods remained a mystery, resisting the efforts of their best analysts. Some proposed she was using the fifth and sixth dimensions to manipulate the components inside the modules. Others scoffed, saying any theory of dimensions beyond the fourth was a myth.*

*Still, no one could deny that she accomplished the impossible, and did it astonishingly fast. Sometime soon, they would introduce her to the Class X objects.*

*One thing they were all agreed on: She must never find out what they were for.*

—

One day, several years into her training, Audrey discovered she could reach farther with her mind than with her fingers. She didn't need to climb the ramps to the top of the tall artifacts or walk back and forth between the ends of the long ones. Her efficiency quadrupled overnight.

Now she began to see how groups of artifacts fit together. Some had missing components, so she cajoled them out of pre-existence and made them be, where they had not been before. This was new.

She was so excited that she forgot how to tire at the end of the day, and spent her free time calling small toys into existence for the younger children in the school.

———

*The government man frowned. "Where is she getting them from? It looks like she's pulling them out of the air."*

*On the other side of the window, Audrey was working on a repair. She had not yet turned their way.*

*"We don't know. They have mass. They exist. Beyond that, we don't know."*

*The left side of his mouth twitched in a sneer. "How do we know they're reliable? They could just pop back out of existence at a critical moment."*

*The teacher's jaw jutted forward. For the barest second, she glared at him. Then she took a slow breath, and her words came out measured and civil. "They never fail. When she fixes things, they stay fixed. It's as if she senses their purpose and gives them what they need."*

*At those last words, his nose twitched, betraying his disgust. Of course the objects didn't really have needs. Or did they? After Audrey finished each day, everything in the room felt inexplicably happier.*

*Audrey turned and saw the teacher. She smiled. Then she saw the government man. She lowered one eyebrow and her head tilted. After a few seconds, she frowned.*

*The man left abruptly.*

———

There was something wrong with the government man. Audrey could feel it. She was glad when he was gone so she could get back to work. A few more pieces and this set of artifacts would be complete.

Audrey's artifacts came to her with numbers on labels. She liked numbers, but they didn't make very good names. Sometimes, for fun, she came up with her own names, knowing instinctively what would fit each object the best. The piece she held now smelled of azure blue, like the number 43 on a spring day. She called it a plandin. The knobs on its sides were not quite even with each other. Audrey could fix that, but she sensed they were happiest that way.

She knew the plandin was created to make music, but no one at the school could hear it except her. She laughed to herself. "Music" was such an inadequate term for something so rich in sensory output.

She lacked the proper appendages to play it the way the Makers would, but she knew how to tease it into performing for her. It tickled her thermoceptors, producing thrilling riffs of warmth with intermittent cool breezes. It twirled around her proprioceptors, making it hard for her to tell where her hands and feet were. Her ears and eyes were barely involved, but somehow she saw beyond the ultraviolet ranges and heard below the lowest bass note. She marveled at the vast range of colors and sounds beyond human perception.

It wasn't just the instruments. The exterior of many of the artifacts glowed with intricate patterns in wavelengths above the human visual spectrum, but oddly included no colors below yellow-orange. Perhaps the Makers were limited as well. Or maybe they just didn't like red.

—

*The government man returned often. He took careful notes as the artifacts were tested and retested. If any of Audrey's parts were to fail — or disappear entirely — it would not escape him. He avoided Audrey herself as much as possible.*

*The teachers whispered about him when he was out of earshot.*

*"Have you seen the way he recoils when she looks at him?"*

*"And then he runs. Always, he runs."*

*"She's exposing his secrets. I know what that's like; she did it to me, too."*

*"But you are not afraid of her. I've seen his face. He looks terrified."*

*"His secrets must be horrific."*

—

Without looking, Audrey saw the government man coming. He was nearly at the door. She knew she made him uncomfortable. She slipped sideways, ducking into dimensions one, two, and five. It made her invisible in regular space. She knew the Makers could occupy four dimensions at the same time, but her human body was limited to three.

After that, she experimented with different combinations. She liked the two-three-five combination. It was actually easier to work from there.

—

*The teachers got accustomed to Audrey disappearing for hours at a time. But her work continued, so they only asked for an explanation.*

*"Where do you go?"*

*"I'm still here."*

*"Why can't we see you?"*

*"I borrow one of the Makers' dimensions. It helps my work."*

*They accepted that. It helped that they were also accustomed to being mystified.*

⁓

The children loved the toys Audrey made, so Audrey made more. In her fifteenth year, she announced to her teacher that she wanted to stop repairing artifacts. She wanted to create.

At first, her teacher couldn't find the words to respond. She stuttered a little, and Audrey waited patiently. She had never asked for time off before. But she was confident that they would agree. How could they not?

"You want a break?" The teacher softened her request to a temporary one. Audrey understood. There were hundreds of artifacts in the storehouses that still needed help, and she might return to them one day. But she had learned all she needed now, and it was time to move on.

She nodded. "I'm tired," she lied, because she knew it would help her teacher justify the change. "I want to help with the children."

Her teacher's face relaxed. Her eyes brightened. "That would be wonderful! You could help find the ones with special talents."

Audrey already knew which ones had special talents. If anyone had asked her, she could have told them. But she knew something else: All children had special potential, if it was nurtured early. She had seen their responses to her toys.

⁓

*"He was mad. Did you see the way he spluttered?"*

*"Yes, but what could we do? It's not as if we could force her to continue."*

*"She never really had a childhood of her own."*

*"How long did he give her?"*

*"A month. But it's not really his choice, is it?"*

⁓

Audrey's new toys and games made it easy for the children to blend their senses. They sorted shades of purple by smell, discovered which numbers itched, and arranged temperatures in order from heavy to light.

The children, unhindered by artificial divisions between "real" and "imagined," eagerly learned all that Audrey taught.

—

*After a month, the government man returned. He insisted that Audrey resume work. Time was getting short, he said. The teachers shrugged.*

*"Would you like to watch her work with the children? They love her."*

*"Can any of them do what she can do?"*

*The teachers exchanged uneasy glances. They had seen the indicators, but none of them wanted to say the words that would take any of the children away from such joyful play. So they resorted to the truth.*

*"There is only one Audrey. Nobody can do what she can do."*

—

Audrey learned to expect a visit from the government man every month. The sixth month, he brought other government people along. Some of them were dressed in uniforms, with decorations on their shoulders and over their pockets.

"Why do they watch us?" the youngest child asked.

"They do not understand."

"Why does he have those ribbons and pins on his shirt?" asked another.

"Some people wear those to make themselves look important."

The little boy started giggling. "That's silly. He's already 'portant, right, Audrey? We're all 'portant."

She gave him a hug.

The children went back to the toys, all except for the oldest child, who stared at the visitors for a long time until they left. Then the girl sat down next to Audrey. The bench was too tall, and she swung her legs. "I wonder…"

"What do you wonder?"

"I wonder how they can be so interested in us, but not at all curious."

"What do you think?"

She sat in silence, pondering. Slowly, her eyebrows rose and her little chin nodded. "I think it's because they are users, not learners, like us."

———

"This cannot continue!" The general's face was red. With each word, he jabbed a finger toward the room where Audrey played with the children. He was new, one of twenty-two people who had come with the government man. "Who is the idiot who let this happen? We are not funding a day care!"

The teacher cringed at his accusations. Then she straightened. "No, but you are funding a school." She stepped toward the glowering man, until her chin almost touched his chest. "And you are disturbing the students."

This was true. The children had stopped playing and were staring.

The man growled. "It's been a year! How much more playtime does she expect?"

The teacher fidgeted, backing away and shuffling her feet. "I don't know."

"You… don't… know." His voice was high-pitched, mocking. "You tell her I want her back on the job first thing tomorrow morning. That's an order. And she's going to fix the Class X artifacts. No more of this namby-pamby stuff."

In the next room, on the other side of the sound-proof window, Audrey looked up. Her gaze, stern and steady, caught his.

He flinched. His entourage parted ahead of him as he hurried to the door. He paused at the threshold and turned. "Tomorrow!" Then he was gone and so were they.

———

Audrey met her teacher at the door, before she had moved more than three steps into the room.

"Audrey, I…"

"I know. Tell him I will meet with him tomorrow. But he will have to bring the High Commander."

She returned to the children. They looked at her, questioning. She weighed her words, and finally, she spoke.

"There's something happening. They're afraid. It's time to finish what we started."

—

"Is she crazy? I can't bring the High Commander. Did you tell her what I said?"

"That was her response. Do you want her to fix it or not?"

—

When the general and the High Commander arrived, the teacher asked, "Do you want me in the meeting?" Her expression said, *Will you be okay alone?*

Audrey smiled. She realized that she was taller than her teacher. When had that happened?

"No, I'll be okay alone."

They stood on opposite sides of the artifact, the young woman facing the two weathered soldiers. It was squarish, with alien designs on its surface. Audrey was surprised to see red and orange markings. She touched the device. It was powerful. Built for destruction.

"You'll fix it?" The general, she noticed, didn't ask her if she could. He believed. He was nervous, but at least he believed.

She nodded. "There is need."

The High Commander stepped back. "Get on with it. I have put my whole day on hold for this."

He turned to the general. "Couldn't you have done this without me?"

She answered first. "No, he could not."

And then she began to reach out with her mind and her fingers. They slipped in and out of dimensions, finding strands, guiding. She sensed the artifact's purpose. Class X, they called it. Destroyer of Worlds. She had never redirected an artifact, but she knew it was possible.

That would have to wait.

An odd hum filled the room, clear and beautiful to those who could hear the music. Now it was not just Audrey. The children were listening too.

She found the strand that was out of place. It stretched tautly from the general to the High Commander and beyond. She knew its name.

"Fear," she whispered. The music took the word and rose, building to a crescendo, spilling over the artifact and the school and the people inside. She felt pity for the men before her. How had they lived, so twisted? She reached to fix them. Fear could be overcome with love.

And then she stopped. Her eyes widened. A threat hovered just outside the system. Fear, she knew instinctively, should not be removed if a threat remained. She searched for its root, reaching to the end of her reach, folding dimensions, sliding through space.

There it was. Just beyond her touch. The root of the threat — and more fear.

The simplicity of it startled her, and she laughed. But still, it was too far to fix, light years away. Perhaps if she focused again.

She was so intent that she felt the touch on her elbow before she sensed them. The children had come. Their sweet music blended with her own, their love boosting hers until she touched it, the edge of the other fear, and the physical distance melted away.

She heard the multiple hearts of the enemy. She cradled their heads in her hands and wiped their tears. They're like us, she marveled. They cherish their children. They lift the fallen. They build for the future.

She could see exactly where the strands should go, even on the war-torn, desperate world of their ancient enemy. Even here, across the Class X artifact, in the souls of the two weary soldiers.

Lovingly, carefully, she wove their strands, all the way from the root. And then she didn't need to sustain the love any longer. It was coming back at her from across the galaxy and from across the room. Freed from fear. Free to love. Purpose dawned across their faces and they smiled.